TO LOVE

(SUCH A BAD IDEA BOOK 1)

DANIELLA BRODSKY

ONE

OLIVIA

Mine is a story as old as the hills: Girl meets boy. Boy takes girl as far across the globe as physically possible. Boy screws secretary on first week cohabitating with freshly emigrated girl. Girl sells all boy's belongings for one dollar on eBay and finds herself stuck *Down Under* with no friends, no family, and no will to confess to the hole she's dug for herself.

Thankfully, I have a job. A very good job. Best one I've ever had. I'm a data geek. As a marketing research analyst, I look at all the facts and figures before big decisions are made, so there are no mistakes.

Yes, the irony of impulsively moving across the world for Mr. Wrong is not lost on me.

But Corey had the bad-boy hair, the stupidly perfect washboard abs, the Australian accent that affected this otherwise conservative, considered small-town American girl, and he was the smartest guy I'd ever met. How was I to know he'd use it for evil?

I trust people. This is my kryptonite. But that ship has sailed.

"Another champagne?" the bartender asks.

I nod, trying to discreetly wipe my buffalo-wing-sauced mouth with a *serviette*, aka a napkin.

I've eaten all but three *chips,* which are called french fries in New York. I swipe all three of them with two fingers and down them with the dregs of my champagne as Steve, the bartender, delicately places a fresh flute of bubbles in front of me.

I'm emotional eating. I'm not above admitting it. And it makes zero sense since I just suffered through the kind of spin class that hurts so badly, five people left early. But I didn't. I fucking stayed. Just so I could binge on two thousand calories, or however many *kilojoules.*

The fat spike did improve my mood for a minute. But it's starting to dip again with a sip of the second champagne, which, despite initial appearances, is nearly flat. I let the liquid pool on my tongue and crane my neck to see what's going on in this *hotel*, which we would call a *bar* back home.

It's packed for a Wednesday at 8:00 p.m., but they're airing the *footy* game starring the local team; half the guys here are wearing lime green jerseys in support, so the crowd makes sense.

There are a lot of group chants: *no!* and *bloody useless!* and *come on, mate!* And I'm starting to smile at the culture of my neighbors in my new home. I think this might be the moment when I have transformed from a visitor to a part of this place. And then I realize it feels pretty damned good, when one scream drowns out the rest, pulling me from my joyful reverie.

"Never again!" It's a woman's voice coming from a table in the far corner under one of the large televisions suspended from the ceiling. Since many eyes are already focused that way, we all witness the tall, thin, wisp of a woman stand, her chair screeching across the floor, and pick up a glass of wine and splash it in the face of the man sitting opposite her.

Everyone applauds and there's a fair amount of laughter.

Good on ya, lass! and a bunch of wolf whistles accompany the woman's exit before everyone goes back to a clearly contentious call in the match.

Except me.

The guy mops liquid from his face and expensive-looking shirt with a bunch of *serviettes*. My first thought is *I'm sure he deserved it*. He doesn't seem too fazed by the woman's departure. He's certainly not going after her, nor is he disputing whatever she must've accused him of.

He's stupidly hot. Like the kind of *bloke* who could steal a girl from any of the Hemsworth brothers without trying.

He catches me looking and flashes a lopsided smile that is less asshole-ish than it should be, given the situation.

I watch as he makes his way to the bar and takes the seat alongside me.

TWO

AIDEN

The girl at the bar looks familiar. In fact, my third neck crane in her direction is what lands that drink in my face. Oh, I had it coming, sure. But she is the straw that breaks the camel's back.

Really, it's awful timing. Sheri, the drink thrower, is meant to accompany me to the conference in two days' time. My father and everyone else is expecting it since I put on that ridiculous song and dance after the last media frenzy over what the headlines love to call my "sexcapades". Let's just say the words *well-hung* most frequently come up with my name in the old Google search thanks to the last woman I made the mistake of sleeping with.

The disappointment in my father's eye at yet another reactive media campaign meeting is the Achilles heel of this otherwise untouchable man, and that's when I made the sweeping oaths about becoming a new man. The gales of laughter from Dad and my brother Finn made me double down, promising I would have a stable relationship by the time this conference rolled around. Neither of them believed me. And that definitely drove me to more ludicrous depths of dedication to the cause.

By now they must be chomping at the bit at the thought of my failure. And so, a man with my agenda should find it easier to concentrate on pretending Sheri is the love of my life, as distasteful as that is to me.

But after the first glance I get of the incredible blonde at the bar, I realize it isn't just recognition that has me drawn to her. There's an unfamiliar stirring. There's attraction, sure. But there's something else I don't recognize. *Real feeling*. No. It couldn't be. That's a fantasy for the innocent and uninitiated, not for someone like me, who's never been in contact with a woman who wants me for anything more than my money and power. Which brings me to the truth about me and women. Regardless of what my father and the tabloids think, my reputation is worse than the reality. I treat people the way they treat me.

I feel bad when I return my gaze and it's clear Sheri's caught me watching the blonde, because I've never looked at *her* like that, like there's no one else, like I'm completely disoriented and needing to ground myself by fitting this woman into my new reality.

Sheri smooths the furrow in her brow, then tries to bring me back with a description of the dresses she's packed for the various dinners at the conference. I have no idea what she's saying.

I tell myself I will not look back at the bar but I only caught the slightest glimpse of the woman's eyes and as I struggle to fill out the image of her in my mind's eye, I can't pin down the exact shade of green—as if I need another piece of evidence that something deeply unprecedented is happening to me from being in the same room with this woman.

So, I look again. This time she's focused on the footy playing on the television suspended above our heads. The Raiders are kicking ass this season and this is an important match for them.

The look on Sheri's face when I suggested we come to this hotel to catch the game was sheer disgust. Michelin chef meals and the couture I've just bought for her conference wardrobe are the bits of our arrangement she's most interested in. But this woman at the bar is watching with interest, looking around the room at the excitement of the crowd as if she's drinking it in. It's gorgeous. I catch the eye color and putting words to it feels absurdly like winning the lottery. *Like looking at a lush valley of eucalyptus trees through a crystal.* This is exactly what I'm thinking when the woman with the apparently mind-scrambling green eyes catches me looking. Her thumb and forefinger go to her lip and she gives a tug. I can't help but smile. It feels like I'm smiling *into* her. The force of it is so strong, she must feel it.

"*Ahem,*" Sheri says, her eyes bulging. This is a woman whose entire life purpose is to be the center of attention, and here I am forgetting she's sitting across from me. "Maybe I should just tell the *Sydney Morning Herald* about our little arrangement," she says. She's the kind of woman who signed a lock-tight nondisclosure agreement at the promise of free designer clothes and a few months of VIP treatment, so I know she's not going to follow through, or she'd have to give it all back.

But no one threatens me. And so, the third time I look at the woman with the crystalline Eucalypt eyes is no accident. It's a conscious pull from the dark side to the intense brightness that familiar, stunning woman at the bar is showering over me.

In her presence, it seems absurd that finding someone to fit the role of suitable girlfriend has been a failure of such epic proportions. *She's right here.*

Insert drink in face. I do my best not to show any reaction. I don't want to give Sheri the satisfaction. Women treat me like a paycheck; lie, cheat, and contort themselves into what they think I want. I can't play into that for long. It's repellent. So, when it doesn't work out, one after another prove with their ugly behavior exactly why I didn't want them in the first place. And here we are again.

I'm honest. And this is where things always blow up. I'm not going to play the games these girls want to play. I'm not going to pretend we're anything other than what we are. I don't see the point. I just wasn't built that way. I've seen firsthand what it leads to.

I wipe my face with my palm as the room cheers for Sheri, who swishes her nonexistent hips dramatically as she makes her exit. I'm glad for the moment to gather myself, though, because my heart is racing from looking directly at Miss Sky Blue Eyes. The gaze I trained on her was so honest that I feel my mouth raise into a half smile, like it's confessing that was all about her.

As I walk up to the majestic woman at the bar—who is eating enough for a footy team, and trying to pass off like it isn't her food, even though she has the cutest little dot of sauce at the corner of her mouth—the feeling I know her, outside of this intensely destabilizing moment we've just shared, is getting stronger.

THREE

OLIVIA

With this gorgeous man smelling like heaven alongside me, I try to watch the football game, but I cannot make heads or tails of what's happening even at the best of times.

"Hungry?" he asks.

I look his way. This close, it's almost off-putting how handsome he is. There is an animal magnetism emanating from him that makes it hard to breathe. *God, imagine if Corey saw me with him* is a thought that pops into my head when I see the way his crisp white shirt hugs his shoulders as he swings his suit jacket over the backrest of the swivel stool. I'm not proud of it. But I can't concentrate on that very long because my eye is drawn to the wet patches that render the material of his shirt sheer, giving me a glimpse of the sculpted chest below.

"Oh, those aren't mine." The bartender hasn't taken them away from the last person." I scrunch my nose and raise my lip in distaste at the pile of licked-clean bones, which I'm trying to pull off as not being mine.

On cue, Steve moseys over from the other side of the bar. "Done with these, love?"

I'm going to kill him.

The guy actually laughs. I try not to notice how this transforms every bit of his face—the creases deepening at his eyes, which glint in the light, the planes of his chiseled cheekbones gliding into a position made for classical sculptors. He gives his hair a scrub with his palm and I try to pretend this has no effect on me.

This man, with his disarming laugh and sparkling eyes, is clearly trouble. I need to put up my guard.

"What are you laughing at, Mr. Wet Shirt?" I arch a brow.

He cocks his head, raises a shoulder, but doesn't offer any kind of explanation.

But I'm curious, so I press on. "Not exactly great with women, huh?"

"Oh, that's not true. Just the opposite, actually. I'm too good with women. It's my kryptonite."

So, we use the same expression? That doesn't mean anything.

And yet I feel myself soften to him and his gorgeousness and his spicy, clean man smell, open to the possibility that in the spectrum of men, he could be more of a lovable cad than a despicable user of women. Not that I care. I'm never trusting one of those—gorgeous or shocking, spicy or sweet—again.

I put my hand to my mouth and realize I have sauce on my face. I swipe at it.

He picks up a serviette and dabs at the spot. I try not to notice the way my face sears white hot at his touch. Or the way the burning spreads to every limb.

"You missed a spot," he says.

FOUR

AIDEN

O h, she responded to my touch. And I like the idea of that. Not just the appearance. This is something new. Dare I say *fun*?

"We both need something stronger," I say. "Besides, looks like your bubbles have gone flat. Whiskey?"

Her face scrunches. "Never drank any before."

Now most women lie around me. They tell me what they think I want to hear. If I say whiskey, they become an expert on malted barley distillation.

"Do you want to try? I'll make sure it's an excellent one, so you give it the best possible chance."

"I like that offer. You can only make choices based on having the right information. Do it."

I call the bartender over and ask if he's got any Lagavulin. It's the best.

He nods and grabs a bottle on the top shelf and pops the cork.

"Two please, neat."

I notice her watch him pour the amber liquor into the two sparkling crystal glasses. Even the most modest pub knows how to serve a good whiskey. I enjoy how my stunning companion focuses on the experience, appreciating instinctively this is something special. I can't remember the last time I relished something like that.

It hits me as the barman slides two beermats in front of us and places the glasses on top of them: I don't know her name.

I pass her a glass and raise mine in her direction. "To the first time Aiden met—" I open my other palm in her direction for her to fill in the blank.

"Olivia." She's wearing the funniest expression. It's like she's charmed, dare I say, *attracted*, and yet trying her damnedest not to be. She's a lip tugger. This is the third time she's done it in the few minutes I've been sitting here.

We clink, and the purest sensation of joy shoots through me as her watery green eyes widen and brighten from the smile at her lips.

I take a sip. It's such incredibly delicious soul-warming stuff, and somehow that feels suited to the occasion.

I watch as she sips—not with trepidation, but slowly all the same, thoughtfully. She lets it swirl around her mouth. I know the way it's thick and rich at first, then finishes with smoky, lingering peat. Perfect. *Like her.*

I'm enjoying her, but I don't know where that thought has come from; I've been around the block long enough to know that no one's perfect. If you could count on people the way you could count on a sixteen-year-old Lagavulin, well, this world would be a totally different place.

She tilts her head, locks her eyes on mine and tugs her lip again. My brain clicks the image for—*for what, exactly?*

"So, what do you think?" I ask. I feel my eyes dancing in sync with hers.

"I've never experienced anything like it. I don't know what I was expecting, but that is—wow."

"I know, right?" Why does this make me feel so stupidly happy?

She takes another sip and closes her eyes this time, trying to place the sensations. It's amazing, sharing this with someone so clearly enjoying it, slipping into this new world of nuanced flavors and sensations.

"It's *massive*," she says, and I think we're both trying not to get too caught up in her word choice. She clears her throat, looking at anything but me. "Not in the same way as one of those big red wines. Deeper than that. Like a bonfire, all consuming."

Sure, hearing her say *massive* and *deeper* has an effect on me. I feel my cock twitch. But beyond that—making the whole thing even more enjoyable—is the way she is *getting* this whiskey thing.

"Is that berry or strawberry I'm getting? Yum. How have I never had this before?"

"Probably because it's $25 a glass."

She—quite unladylike—spits some of that $25 of Lagavulin onto the bar. So, she doesn't come from money. A sneaky way to work that into the conversation, but I'm glad I did. Another point for her. Not that she's trying to score points. In fact, I think it's quite the opposite.

And then I remember where I know her from.

FIVE

OLIVIA

I remember Corey giving me a hard time when I asked for new champagne at a bar to replace one that was flat or had gone off. That's a point for Mr. Wet Shirt. Then the whiskey—the way he thoughtfully delivered me into the experience of it with him, like he wanted more than anything to see me enjoy it.

Well, that's something new. Something wonderful, actually. And the atmosphere created by his pleasure tips the world on its side. And from here everything looks different.

I'm not sure if that influences how delicious the Lagavulin is, but jeez, that stuff is incredible. Like the portal to another universe dripping in wow. It's just a drink. Sure, I know that. But with the low I've been in for the past couple of months since the Corey debacle and the pressure of keeping up the facade that my Australian boyfriend and I are doing well and we're excited for my parents' trip next month, well, this shift in perspective yields some power.

I still don't have a solution to the problem of how I'm going to break my parents' hearts. Again. A final blow, most likely, after the song and dance I delivered to assure them I'd be safe here. But I feel more hopeful than I have since Corey's firm ass pounding into that redhead was branded onto my brain. And that has to mean something.

SIX

AIDEN

I know where she's from. She's the new girl. The data girl. And she's here because of me. I told dear old Dad we needed to build up our data team, that data was the way of the future, and this girl was going to be my ticket to proving it.

Her reputation preceded her, and I made her an offer ten times what anyone else would pay because I had to have the best if I was going to get this right. And the way you find the best is by talking to people who know how she works, how she made all that cash for that big American fashion brand that will remain nameless because they did not appreciate what she'd done. I will not make that mistake—the generous salary is only the beginning. Successful business is all about loyalty and anyone who works for P.I.C. knows that.

We have recruiters who know how to find the people behind the people—the people who get shit done, not the ones who take all the credit. And she's the real deal. I hadn't met her yet. I don't usually work with people at that level; we're up on our own floor. I only recognize her from her headshot. I swear, there was glitter hovering above the surface of that print. She's just that kind of woman.

But surely she knows who I am. I'm always in the gossip pages for all the wrong reasons. And that little wine in the face trick is probably jogging her memory. True, she's just come here. So, there is a chance she may not have encountered my reputation yet. If there *is* a God, anyway. I'm going to give her the benefit of the doubt on that point. She hasn't done anything to show me she deserves anything less.

"I think I know you," I say. "You work at P.I.C., don't you?"

"Yeah, yeah I do. Do you? I'm pretty sure I'd remember you." I don't think she notices the way her fingers twist in her hair, but *I* certainly do.

"I do, yeah. But I don't think we've met."

"Oh." She looks dubious. It looks hot on her.

I don't know how to say it. I don't want to tell her who I am, and yet, I have to, don't I? Why don't I want to tell her? Is that *hope* I feel beneath that attraction? Shit. All right, I better just be out with it.

"Aiden Wheatley." I offer my hand, the one that's gained me the title of *The Firmest Handshake in Finance.* People like to use sexual innuendos with my name, keep up the hype that sells those papers. Not that there's *nothing* to it.

"Aiden Wheatley?" Her brow furrows adorably. "You're the son of the company founder."

I can only imagine the click-clacking of her putting those pieces together.

"The one and only."

She sips at the Lagavulin, licks her lips before she catches herself and darts her eyes to see if I noticed. *Yup.*

"Oh, I've heard about you." Lip tug.

Here we go.

"Well, you can believe what you want to believe, I guess." I shrug.

She's caught again, this time looking at my shoulders. Can't

blame the woman, can I? I'm sure my look is just as desirous.
She's irresistible. Worth getting that drink thrown at me, just to
see her enjoying the view of my chest through the wet, see-
through bits of my shirt. I want to say that and take her face in
my hands.

"Are you saying it's not true?" The pronounced apples of
her cheeks are calling out for me to touch.

"Well, I don't know what you've heard." I take a long drink,
swallow as her eyes trace my Adam's apple, then let my tongue
dart out. You could carve the attraction between us. And with
my track record, that'd probably end up derailing my plan to
have Data Girl bring P.I.C. into a new level of profit.

"I think you might."

I smile. She's smart. "Do you read gossip magazines or the
finance pages?"

"I don't really read gossip magazines," she says. "But I do
scan the finance pages daily. It's my job."

"You're the data girl."

"I'm the data girl."

"*Data Girl.*" I'm so distracted by the image of me whis-
pering that into her ear as I drive into her that I don't realize I've
growled it like that, out loud, until her eyes bulge and her head
darts back.

Slow down, man. At least I won't tell her it was me who
brought her here. "How are you liking it so far?"

She nods, too vigorously. "Good, really good." She sips her
whiskey.

"You don't strike me as data girl."

"What's a data girl supposed to look like?"

"Oh, you know. Ponytail, big glasses. No makeup, *daggy*
clothes."

"I'll try better."

"Please don't."

There's that smile again. Not only does it take me back to the image of our skin sliding and our bodies colliding, but the sight of her lips in a curl brings on one thought, clear as day: I like her. I really like her. That doesn't happen every day. People in general disappoint me.

"Want to try another whiskey? I'll give you a different one this time: Laphroaig."

"Bit more than I usually drink." She holds her glass up to the light, tips the dregs to one side, then the other before lowering it and cradling it in both hands on her lap.

Oh boy, that image certainly has an effect on me.

"Come on. You're in Australia now. You've gotta keep up."

"Is that a good thing?"

"It's just a thing." I can feel my smile. It's genuine. I want her to know that.

"Okay."

"You have somewhere better to go?"

"Nah." It takes every ounce of self-control not to trace that plump cheek apple.

The bartender pours us another round. Olivia indulges herself. A bit more audibly this time. Probably loosening up from the strength of the scotch whiskey. She audibly shows her enjoyment, making comparisons, and an aural memory I won't soon forget.

"This one is sweeter, has more smoke."

She's right. Again, I note how immensely I enjoy her enjoyment . . . maybe more this time. Sip after sip, she has another insight to the taste and sensation, or an intelligent question, or makes one of those delicious sounds.

She's the one who suggests the third. But she does ask for my advice, and I give it to her. "Let's try an Australian one," I say. "Two Sullivan's Cove, sir."

The bartender tips his head and runs a cloth over two of

those fancy glasses to shine 'em up real nice for this twelve-year-old French Oak barreled liquid gold.

"Australians may not always be the first to the game, but we certainly perfect it. Wait until you try this one." Shit, I was enjoying myself. Before I knew it, it was after midnight.

When Olivia can't quite put her finger on the flavors she's experiencing, we laugh over a description of the whiskey we find online. "A big, fat, chewy single malt full of rich toffee and molasses." She's the one who does the double eyebrow raise. I laugh so loud at our innuendo—equally childish and poking close to the lust sizzling between us—I nearly snort.

"I'm having a really good time," I say when we catch our breath.

"Me too," she says with the kind of sigh that makes me think this hasn't always been the case.

"Can I say something crazy?" I ask.

"Oh no. I knew this was too good to be true." She's already shaking her head, her body tensing. "What is it?"

"Well, I know you don't know much about me, but you seem to have heard some stuff."

"Yeah." She's on the edge of her high swivel chair, uncrossing her legs and lowering her feet to the ground.

"Well, there's a company-wide conference coming up."

"Oh yeah. I'm going to that conference." She lets out a breath, with some relief. Which might be premature, given what I'm about to say.

"Aha, well, there's half of my request." I smile, trying to bring her back to the cocoon of us we'd been inhabiting all this time.

"You're making requests?"

"Why don't we call it a proposal if you like that better."

She squints but does seem to prefer that term because she dips her chin for me to finish.

"I need to be at this conference and my father has turned it into something of a deadline for me." *What in the name of all that is holy are you doing bringing this woman into all this, Aiden? And if you are going to* propose *this ridiculous business, then why not tell the truth—that you put this pressure on yourself? There's a whole pile of issues you're not dealing with, and your answer is to bundle them all up and light a match.* But I picture the two of us bypassing all the bullshit and spending more time like this together and something about it feels right— in a way the dumb fake-relationship plan never had a chance of doing with Sheri. That was grueling, painful, and made me feel like the worst kind of imposter. *This,* this feels like the world placing an opportunity to get to know the most intriguing, beguiling woman I've ever met, in a way unlike any other.

She crosses her arms. "*This* is getting interesting."

"Unfortunately, it's not a drama film; it's my life." *No, this* woman *is your life. And you're starting it by misleading her.* And yet, something is drawing me to do this. It's almost as if I have no choice, as if the vacancy in this ridiculous farce was created just so we could be together, skipping all of the bullshit and jump right in.

"I can't tell you how many times I've had that thought." I'd have to hear more about that. But for now, I'm glad that she softens and I can see she's coming back to me.

"Come on, out with it, billionaire." She uses that word like a weapon, something I feel a bit ashamed of. I like that.

"I need to be appearing to have a stable relationship by this conference." *Need or* want? Same thing, I tell myself.

"Oooooh." She laughs. "Wet shirt?" She looks at me from beneath splayed fingers. It's adorable. I want to pull her into my arms, especially when she's looking at them like candy in a display window.

"Wet shirt." I smirk.

"Surely you have a backup plan? Another chick you can take to the conference to pretend she's into you. She might even *be* into you."

"All true. However—"

"Yes?"

"I need it to be someone special."

She tries to pretend that doesn't mean anything to her, but I can tell it does. We've both been here these past couple of hours that have brought us closer than several decades of my life have done with anyone else. Olivia rolls her eyes, shakes her head. All the visual signs of dissent are there, but they're hollow.

"Someone smart, who can hold her own. I need you." I place my hand on hers. She looks at where our skin meets. I'm sure she feels the current running between us, too.

"*Me?* You want me to pretend I'm dating you?"

"Oh, no, no, no. Not just *dating* me, that you're serious enough to accept a marriage proposal."

Again, with the spitting. A spitter. She's a spitter. And somehow, even this is sexy. Her lack of guise.

"Sorry," she says, covering her mouth. "But you're kidding, right? This is an actual life. Two lives, actually—your life and my life. I mean, I've been in some bad relationships, but this, my friend, smells like disaster."

"Don't tell me you haven't had fun tonight?" She's authentic. She won't lie.

"You're right, I have. Actually, I've had more fun than I've had since I got here."

"Well, somebody's clearly not showing you the right spots. You come with me and I'll show you an Australia you'll never want to leave."

"You know, I'm new to this bargaining thing, but I can tell that's not a very even deal."

"So, what is it you want? Go ahead, name your price."

"Hmmmm." She pretends to think, but it's clear she already has something in mind. "I've got a tricky situation of my own." She shakes her head and tosses a palm, but it still doesn't seem like she's taking it seriously, like this is just some kind of flirting we'll forget about with the next whiskey.

Then she seems to realize what she's saying, goes rigid. "No. Never mind. This is crazy. Forget the whole thing. We can't do this. Aside from how just *Three's Company*-zany the whole thing is, you also happen to be my *boss*."

"Oh, come on. At least tell me what you were going to say. I've shown you so much—big, fat, chewy single malt? Come on. Even if you're going to say no. Be honest here. If nothing else, I think we've—we've started something. We're friends, honest people who enjoy each other's company. Can you at least say that?" *Friends, my ass. Honest?* If there was a God, I'd be smited for that, but there's definitely something between us: that part is real as they come, and I tell myself the ends justify the means.

She nods. Then collapses into herself, lips fluttering. "All right, well, I came to Australia because I was in a relationship with somebody, and I moved all the way across the world to keep him. It's the reason I accepted your offer." There's something wordy and circuitous to her phrasing that's different to every other sentence she's uttered tonight. *Keep him.* I hate that choice of words passing though her lush lips, and it doesn't jive with the way she's presented herself tonight. This is not a woman who struggles to *keep* a man, this is a goddess whom men throw themselves over hot coals for. She knows that, and still there's something about her that says she doesn't trust it. And I have the urge to protect her so she never doubts herself again.

She uses her fingers like a plane going down, sound effects and everything. "And the first week Corey and I were living together, I came home to find him screwing someone in our bed.

Hadn't even slept in it two nights. I'm not going to make excuses —I own it—but it was the stupidest thing I've ever done."

"Give me his number. I'll fucking kill him."

She smiles hugely, like no one else had offered. Looking at her, I find that hard to believe.

"Thank you. But that's not going to solve anything. My parents are coming here in a month. And after a lifetime of worrying about me because . . . well . . . because I'm their daughter, obviously, they've used all their savings to buy tickets to come and see me and the happy life their only daughter went so far away from them to find. They're gonna be devastated. I just can't even bring myself to hurt them that way."

Oh, there is more to unpack there.

"So, you pretend for me and I pretend for you. What's the harm? I just pretend I'm the one who swept you off your feet and showed you there's a better man than Corey. You're gonna find someone else in no time after they've had their lovely trip and feel confident you're in good hands. I'm sure I'll be better than Corey anyway. He sounds like an absolute wanker. And then when you put them back on the plane, they'll be happy as clams. Problem solved. Who's it gonna hurt?" I give a half shrug, as if every bit of me isn't on tenterhooks waiting for her to agree.

"Forget it."

SEVEN

OLIVIA

O h, I say *no* a good fifteen times. But the whole time, I keep picturing Mom and Dad with Aiden starring as the new Corey, and you know what I see? Complete happiness. And if I'm being honest with myself it's not just my parents joy I'm envisioning. But I'm not going to let this head-turner part me from my senses just because I can't seem to think straight in his presence.

I leave out the part where Mom and Dad worry about me so much because I spent my whole childhood sick—in and out of hospitals. I nearly blurt it, but save myself, thank God. I've been healthy for years, put a lot of effort into my health (despite tonight's gorge fest), and I don't see how that's relevant if Aiden is only proposing to this role playing for a limited run.

But that's why it is so hard to tell them the truth. They were terrified of me leaving for another country, researched the best private health coverage and made me secure doctors, and send them my entire medical history, which is quite long, since it started when I was born two months premature at just over one pound. All this before I'd even stepped foot on the Australian continent. If they knew I was here by myself, with no one to help me if something went wrong, well, *oh boy*.

And the truth is, I could have gone home immediately after I the image of Corey pumping away into the girl with the flame-red hair was permanently burned into my retinas, but I didn't want to.

The second I sipped my first *long black* coffee, went to my first incomprehensible *footy match*, drank my first Coonawara Shiraz, I knew this was a world I wanted in on. I loved the warmth of *mateship*, the richness of the convict history, the vast-ness of the land, the haunting beauty of the Aboriginal art and culture—so poignant and lasting.

I'm a fate person. I am *Data Girl*, after all. And yet, I couldn't shake the pressing sense of destiny about my being here in *Aus* (pronounced "Oz"). Maybe it's the scotch whiskey talk-ing, but tonight, the intensity of that fateful sensation that somehow I'd landed where I *belong* increases a thousand-fold looking into those crystal blue eyes, the permanent line etched above Aiden's nose as he looks at me with the full weight of destiny—like he feels it too. Which is crazy.

And exactly the kind of thing you do not allow yourself to act on, regardless of the intensity. It's the kind of thing you try your hardest to laugh at, ridicule into the disbelief portion of your brain.

"Well, let me get you home safe, at least."

"Fine," I say, half-hoping he'll make me agree to this crazy plan by the time we reach my building.

"Will you at least sit with me at the conference? Have meals at my table?"

"Why not?" I raise a bare shoulder. "I'd enjoy making all the female—and half the male—employees jealous."

He smiles that wolfish grin that's been working its magic on me all night. I think he suspects he's getting closer to agreement from me.

We're walking on the seedy part of Oxford Street, which is nothing compared to the seedy parts of Manhattan—just a few brow-raising signs advertising the kinds of dance parties I've certainly never been invited to.

My place is in a small, but beautiful new building in the jaw-droppingly cool Surrey Hills suburb. I "negotiated" the parting with Corey by kicking his ass out, so I kept the apartment—which we'd prepaid six months' rent for.

It's remarkable, the way Aiden inches closer to me as we pass the gritty club. Our shoulders bump and we both turn to each other. A second passes in which I would surely agree if he asks me. Probably, I would agree to nearly anything he wants of me.

Aiden parts his lips. It feels incredibly erotic—my eyes fix there as the rest of the world goes blurry. He grabs my hand. My chest flutters. His thumb rubs like an explorer of a new continent and suddenly my body goes up in flames.

"What do you say?" he says, stopping suddenly, holding us at the spot. We've just turned the corner to my street. We're under my favorite tree—a cherry blossom that's just bloomed, as if there's a stage director who's arranged it. "Will you be my girlfriend?"

"Fake girlfriend, you mean."

"Right." The intensity of his eyes is knee-buckling.

My body goes limp. He's got me. Despite the numbers that would certainly point to disaster, I hear myself agree. "Yes, let's do it." I put out my other hand to shake. He takes it, and now both my hands in his, he pulls me in.

Chest to chest, our lips are so close. In the light of the street-lamp, the planes of his face are perfectly shaded, a whisper of a five o'clock shadow ratcheting the whole thing up to deadly sexy. Beneath the intensity, a hint of playfulness shines through.

Aiden gently places his hand on my chin and pulls my lips to his, stopping short of contact. "We should seal it with a kiss, no?"

"I can't see what other way would work." I don't recognize this Olivia, but I like her style.

Our eyes dance as if there's so much we're not saying. There's pure joy in his eyes. I'm sure of it. And if the way I'm feeling is reflected in my own gaze, it's a perfect match for his. With natural chemistry like this, how hard will it be to pretend?

Slowly, he closes the final distance between us. My eyes close in the sensation of his strong lips on mine. The second I feel them, I want more. His hands are on my hips, pulling me close. It's a tsunami of sensation. I feel my lower half press into him. He growls and I think, *oh my*, I can only imagine where this would go if I let it.

I don't know how I'm going to pull away, but just as I'm trying to work up to it, Aiden holds my bottom lip between his, then lets me go.

I shiver. As he retreats, I'm staring at his mouth. I want it back.

"This is going to be good," he says. "I think this is the perfect arrangement."

Is it me, or is he being purposefully obtuse in his language choice? He could mean the faking-it deal or a relationship between the two of us. And me? Which would I prefer? Faking it, obviously. Wouldn't trust the man as far as I can throw him.

And I'd have serious trouble throwing this one. He's so . . . *so*.

He walks me into the foyer of my building, waits for the elevator to ding and its doors to slide open, then pulls me inside, as close as he can to him so that every part of me is melding to every part of him, then he covers my lips in his again and lusciously kisses me. It's pure lust. But that hand at the back of my neck? *Professional*, I tell myself. He's sliding right into the role.

EIGHT

AIDEN

Two days later, I'm on the private jet with Dad and a couple of assistants tapping away incessantly at laptops. I sometimes wonder if they're actually working that hard or checking their Facebook profiles. What is their motivation?

Money, I remind myself. Without the urgency of that basic need, life is different. I'll be the first to acknowledge that.

"I cannot wait to meet this girlfriend of yours, Aiden. I have to admit," my father says, "I didn't think you'd be able to meet that deadline you set." He raises his short black coffee to his lips.

A vision of Sheri pouring a drink on me at Olivia's serendipitous head-turning presence at the Grand Hotel flashes. If it hadn't been for that, I'd be here with a woman I didn't care a toss for, lying and feeling like shit. Instead, all the untruths are about the details. The feelings are undeniably real. And it makes me sit up straighter, feel *more* in his presence. How can Olivia—in one night—have made such a difference in me? I don't know the answer, but the overwhelm of my senses that caused me to propose Olivia take Sheri's place in this scheme amounted to the right reasons—and it makes the world look like a different place.

"When have I missed a deadline?" I ask.

"That's true. But you've never had one that had to do with your behavior with women. That is a real challenge for you, I know."

One of the assistants wordlessly places a folder on the table in front of my father.

"I could say the same to you."

"Touché."

Bless these assistants. They don't bat an eye. Non-disclosure agreements and shut-the-fuck-up salaries help with that kind of thing. But they know the truth better than anyone.

Most sons would probably have nothing to do with fathers who screwed so many women behind their mother's back, but my mother was an absolute saint and she found the strength to guide and navigate a relationship with me and Dad that no other woman would have done.

She wanted us to have this. She knew that despite my father's many, many faults, that he was a bona fide genius who had a lot to teach me, and a natural connection to me that made him want to do so.

And years later, she really has left all that in the past. She's happy, rich from an obscene divorce settlement, and in love with a man who actually deserves her. Mum's actions have taught me just as much as her words.

I wish I could say Dad's aged badly and learned the error of his ways, but that would be a lie. Women flock to him. He runs a multi-billion-dollar company he's going to hand off to me in a few years. "If you get your reputation in order," he's fond of saying. We both know I'm getting the company no matter what, but his respect? Well, that's a different—and more important— thing entirely. And if he isn't exactly the kind of person you'd slap a *happy* label on, he's still living his life and sucking every bit he wants out of the marrow. No regrets as far as I can see. Except for me. But I'm going to change that.

"So, tell me about this woman," Dad says. "Why haven't we met her if I'm to believe this is serious?"

Because I didn't know her until a couple of days ago. "Would I be bringing her to dine with our family otherwise?" Not our thing. *Until Olivia.* We bond over business deals, celebrate with world-class whiskey, then go our separate ways. Mostly to women's beds. *Like father, like son.* Heard that plenty of times. But it isn't true. We aren't the same at all.

Dad nods, palms his chin. "So?"

"Olivia works for P.I.C."

"Oh, no wonder you pushed for that rule about dating being allowed as long as it's not a direct superior."

"Hadn't even known she existed then." I'm picturing her glowing green eyes. How could I ever have been ignorant of her existence?

"You work fast, then!"

"When you know, you know," I say. Surprisingly, I find there's weight to that. Olivia is the perfect person for this arrangement. *And perfect for other stuff, too.*

"I'm sure it's a relationship built to last—despite a world of evidence to disprove the existence of such a thing." Dad sits back, rearranges himself into another power pose. He doesn't do it on purpose. This is just who he is. Never been in a situation where a person didn't do what he said. Except with Mum, that is.

"Well, Olivia would have something to say about that. She's a data girl."

"Ah, well, it's all beginning to make sense now—your push to beef up the research department."

"Nope. Nothing to do with her. But when you meet her,

you'll start to understand—both why this is the way of the future and why she's the woman to take us there."

"I barely recognize you, son. If I didn't know better, I'd think you were putting it on."

I don't flinch.

The flight out to the Hunter Valley is a little over thirty minutes. Thankfully, the keyboard tappers pull Dad's attention away from me and my fake girlfriend because I've got some studying to do.

The biographical spreadsheet Olivia gave me is a work of art if you appreciate data, and it gives me an insight into her that far outweighs the stats, like her being born at St. Luke's Hospital in Braidwood, Connecticut, at three o'clock in the morning, twenty-seven years ago, on a Sunday in the middle of a heat-wave, which knocked out all the electricity on the United States' eastern seaboard.

This phenomenal start to life landed baby Olivia, bundled in striped swaddling, fluff of hair fine as silk, on the front page of *The Hartford Courant*, a link to which she'd efficiently embedded in her fake girlfriend dossier. The photo does something that puts the feeling of the term *stopped my heart* into my realm of experiences.

This tidy, comprehensive compilation of facts shows how she sees this—business minded. And that's exactly what I need. So why do I feel more than a little disappointed at this approach of hers?

NINE

OLIVIA

"Olivia Barker?" The receptionist at the hotel repeats my name as she touch types it, and then an inexplicable procession of other keys before she speaks again. "Yes. I have you in the presidential suite with Mr. Aiden Wheatley."

I nearly stumble backward. We're sharing a *room*. We are *sharing* a room. *Sharing a room?* Of course, we are. We're meant to be dating and we're not in junior high school. And he's a world-famous womanizer. And I just used the word *womanizer*. And this womanizer nearly wore me down the other night at the hotel, then again outside my apartment, but I have my wits about me now. Fool me once, shame on you and all that.

"Yes, that's correct." I try to keep my hands from trembling despite the fact those said wits are already unraveling upon hearing this bombshell.

I thought I'd prepared. In fact, I stayed up all night Saturday putting together a spreadsheet with my background so Aiden and I would seem legit.

I'd even done some homework on him. I'm sorry I did. Because the truth is Friday night left me with a lot of questions. This is all meant to be fake and yet when no one was watching we kissed and then we kissed again. And it was hot. And the way my body had reacted was quite a shock.

Every Google entry about him after the several thousand in which he is referred to as "well-hung" was either of women drooling over how sexy he is or a warning to stay away. At the grand old age of thirty, I think Aiden's dated 50 percent of Australian women under the age of thirty and an additional 5 percent of the international wealthy female jetsetters of the same age demographic.

So, by the time I boarded the plane full of P.I.C. employees, a new version of Aiden had already overtaken whatever chemical reaction our amazingly easy talk, fun interaction, and sexy kiss had set off. And I was going to protect myself from him at all costs. Even if my mind kept trying to put an image to exactly what *well-hung* Aiden would look like.

And when the seatbelt light dinged off, and I leaned my chair back all the way in my very first first-class seat, I thought I was in a much better mindset to pull off this fake relationship. I shed any romantic notions that it had been some kind of magical meeting. Or that he had anything to do with my being in first class.

"Another champagne, Ms. Barker?"

"I'd better not," I said. I had to keep my wits about me and that meant not getting all excited about the first-class ticket Aiden had—despite my wanting to believe he hadn't—most likely upgraded me to. I told myself again it was nothing personal to him. But I had trouble believing this. *If it was him, then why did he do it?* Because he knows how to make a business transaction run smoothly. And that's what this is.

Now as I accept the key to the presidential suite, I wonder if he was buttering me up for this massive bombshell. The bellman takes my bag and disappears to some secret employee lift, so I'm only carrying the oversize handbag I use for travel. I step inside the elevator and try to wrestle the key card into the slot to power up the special oval gold button for the presidential suite.

It doesn't seem to be working, so I pull it out and reinsert, when once again the doors slide open. It's Poppy, who is technically my boss, but only because the data team is new and temporarily located within Office Management, which she manages.

Poppy doesn't understand data and doesn't think it's important. In her mean girl way, she's made no bones about that. I'm guessing that has something to do with the fact that as my supervisor, she saw my salary, and if it's anything like industry standards, it's a hell of a lot larger than hers.

She looks at the card and the button I'm pressing, and her nostrils actually flare. I didn't know that was a genuine thing. I'd read about it, but shit, it's scary in person.

I think she'll leave it there, but Poppy isn't a fan of traditional decorum. "*You* are in the presidential suite? How is that possible?"

I decide I'm not going to answer that. Surely, it was meant rhetorically.

It's deathly quiet—the elevator is not even the dinging kind—as we ride up three floors to Poppy's room. She walks across the threshold when the doors open, and I'm about to breathe a sigh of relief when she blocks the door with her hand. There's an oversize gold ring on her index finger in the shape of a very famous and expensive monogram, and it *thunks* against the metal in a way that sends shivers up my spine.

"I don't trust you," she says.

Just stay quiet, I tell myself. But it's too late. Trust is quite a serious topic with me, and clearly, I'm incapable of keeping mum. "The feeling's mutual," I say.

She's gobsmacked and lets her hand drop. The nostrils have started quivering by the time the doors roll closed between us.

This is a terrible start. How did Aiden and I think we were going to get away with this? Just because it's not legally a problem doesn't mean it's not all kinds of wrong. He runs the company where I just started. And clearly, there are opinions about my being here already in place. What is going to happen when it's announced we're in a serious relationship?

Was this a giant mistake? If I get fired, I will have to go home, and I refuse to disappoint my parents that way. And besides, I am not done here in Australia. I think back to the way I felt that night at the hotel—that moment before a woman threw her drink at the man who is now pretending to be my boyfriend.

That was peace, perhaps even joy I felt in feeling like I fit in with a bunch of people watching *the footy*. And—this bit is terrifying—in the moments following, Aiden and I transformed from strangers to something that felt more in line with the connection that seemed to exist between us from the moment our eyes met. It was magical. And I want more of all of that. Something deep down tells me I need it. So, mistake or not, I'm forging ahead.

Thankfully he's not inside the room when I get there because I know seeing him is going to throw me off and my heart is already pounding from that exchange in the elevator. The suite is absolutely gorgeous—classic, like the whole estate. Everything looks handmade and about two hundred years old. There's a marble fireplace and detailed woodwork along all the doorways. The ceiling is vaulted with beams running across, and it feels like I stepped into another time.

The view overlooks the vineyards and the hills beyond in perfect orientation for a stunning sunset. There's a veranda, and before I realize, I'm picturing the two of us out there clinking whiskeys and watching the sun throw shades of pink, blue, and purple across the sky. If there is a way for a place to say that everything's okay, this is it.

And just as a backup, there's that frisson of joy again. And I refuse to ignore it. Even Data Girl knows the importance of instinct. Numbers are just black boxes if we don't know what to do with them, and if life teaches us anything, it's a hard-earned sharpening of our instincts.

This is something with data behind it after all. We are animals and our species wouldn't have survived this long without this intuitive understanding of what's required for our survival.

I turn my gaze to the rest of the suite. There is a living room and kitchen, his and her bathrooms, and yet only one bed. It's massive, but that's not going to change the fact that we're meant to be sharing it. Why had I not considered this? And where does my instinct play into that conundrum? It's staying infuriatingly mum.

I don't want to think about what that means because I've already made the mistake of letting my feelings carry me away— all the way to this sunburnt country. And I'm so not doing *that* again. *Says the woman in a room she's sharing with her fake boyfriend/real boss.*

I step out onto the balcony and Aiden enters the room. He's rolling his own small suitcase, which surprises me, and with a quick scan of the room, he comes upon me immediately. I feel the air change as soon as he's in it. My senses crackle with the idea that I'm about to be close to him. I hadn't accounted for that reaction.

He joins me in the slightly cooling air of early evening in a charcoal suit that hugs every bit of him perfectly, his muscular arms tugging at the shoulders. His crisp white shirt is open at the neck and he isn't wearing a tie. I try not to let my eyes linger too long on the bit of his chest I can see.

Now my instinct makes an appearance. It wants my lips to press against his and feel those strong arms close around me.

"Hello," he says as he leans on the railing alongside me. "Glad you got here safely."

"I did, and thanks for the upgrade." Despite myself, I had to know the facts.

"Well, I wouldn't let my girlfriend fly economy."

Girlfriend. Coming from his lips, the word has the strangest effect on me. There go my fingers tugging on my lip. Of course, he notices.

I'm not playing this cool and that is not acceptable to me. I'll have to kick it up a notch.

"Or sleep in a separate room," I say, one eyebrow hiked.

"Yes, the sleeping arrangements. Are you okay with sharing the room?"

The way he says it, I feel stupid arguing, like I'm not sophisticated enough to share a room with an absolute stranger I'm pretending to be in a serious relationship with. This logic doesn't make any sense, but none of this makes sense.

I don't answer right away, and he must sense my hesitation because he says, "I'll sleep on the floor, of course. Like a gentleman." But the way he says *gentleman* is a little dirty. And *I like it.*

I nod, because I don't trust myself to speak at this second. But then I have a thought. "What about that sofa in the living room?"

"Too small."

Shit, he's right. It's just a two-seater. He'd never fit that incredible body on that miniscule thing.

He sits on one of the woven chaises and uses his palm to rub the back of his neck. His eyes close with the sensation of rubbing the tight muscles.

Combined with the aftershock of our exchange and the one

bed in the room, I feel a sexual thrum vibrate through me. This man is my boss, I remind myself. This is a professional exchange of services and getting romantic for real isn't going to do me any favors. *Well, those kisses you shared say something quite the opposite. Do not tug that lip. Oh, for the love of God, you're doing it again!*

He catches it. One side of his mouth quirks in a lopsided grin.

AIDEN

The conference is not a bullshit lovefest with trust exercises and hollow agreements to upskill and work better as a team. Dad knows that the key to retaining loyal, dedicated employees is to make them feel like they are part of something they want to be a part of. It's the first business lesson he taught me way back in high school.

We secure sought-after speakers and world-class influencers each year to take things to another level for every single employee—no matter the department or seniority. People look forward to it. There's a zeitgeist that starts building months before the date. A marketing team helps with that.

This year the tagline is #bebetter. It's already gone viral. This morning everyone gets a swag bag with that slogan on everything from coffee cups to high fashion yoga pants. In fact, having a P.I.C. conference on your resumé is the kind of thing that can land you a job, separate you from the competition.

One of the most popular events is the open mic Q&A— when anyone can ask my father and me any question they like. Accessibility was the theme about three years ago and it was great. How can you perform to your best standards if you can't get the answers you need? In the months following that conference, we improved our revenue by fifteen percent. These are the kinds of numbers people literally kill for.

The four-day gathering is also good fun. Top shelf booze, Michelin starred chefs, and a party so glamorous on the last night, it would give any Oscar shindig a run for its money.

Of course, last year, that party landed me in some serious trouble—the kind that made me dedicated to showing Dad I am better than that. And maybe myself too, though I wouldn't say that out loud. But this year is going to be perfect. I have the perfect woman for the job. And here she is on the balcony of our room, acting like she wants me to sleep on the floor. Which, of course, is what makes her perfect.

Let me be clear: I wouldn't have it any other way. I *am* a gentleman when the situation calls for it. And I have no intention of screwing this up. However, what "this" is has become unclear.

Her green eyes are liquid, and I drown in them every time I look too long. It was good to have a couple of days away from her to refocus on what I was trying to do with this charade, *Impress your father,* I told myself, but the second I saw her on the terrace, I knew that was only a tiny part now that Olivia was in the picture. She'd changed everything.

I'd asked myself many times before, when I had falsely given the impression I was in a serious relationship, what was I planning to do *after* the conference? Gradually let the relationship go? Assume I'd changed everyone's POV on Well-Hung Aiden Wheatly and they'd forget? And then I could simply go back to being me, but be using more discretion about my sordid sex life?

The truth was I wanted to actually fix it. And that's why I'd left the plan open-ended. Because I *wanted* to change. And I'd thought this new well-hung dedicated boyfriend reputation might just make me man up and do it. But looking at Olivia on the terrace, more beautiful than that world-class backdrop behind her, looking all proper in her business attire, trying to be professional about all this, I realize I'd never really believed that before Olivia came on the scene.

All I know is that I have managed to arrange a lot of time for us to get to know each other, and at the moment, there isn't much I can bring myself to care about more than that.

I'm sitting on the chair, trying to remember what the world looked like when I was entertaining the idea of bringing Sheri here. That now seems impossible when I know Olivia is in the world, I think, when I see her following my hand on my neck like it's something X-rated. And her eyes on me like that make it feel that way. And though I'm a gentleman, I am still a *man*.

I can barely remember what I was going to say. She tugs on her lip and we both take a second. It's undeniable. We both feel it and she knows I know she's feeling it. I tell myself I can keep this under control. So what if the one woman who can do the job of impressing upon Dad that I'm a changed man is the one who's actually punctured the armor? Surely there's no danger in that. There will be more where she came from. *Right. And then I will sprout wings and fly.*

"We don't have anything on for a couple of hours. Should we go over our histories? A little quiz, if you will."

"Sure," she says. "Ask me anything. I've been studying our love story, and I have to say, you're in the wrong industry. You should be a romance novelist. Well done."

I smile in a way I've heard called *roguish*. I've also been told of the effect it has.

From the way her cheeks blush, I can see it still works. I should be putting a damper on all that, I know I should. But something about Olivia makes me lose control.

I lead the way back into the room, my pulse pounding, and pull out her incredible spreadsheet—color coded, bolded, italicized; shit, she knows how to make her data sing. I say so over the ruckus inside my body.

"That's what you hired me for," she says.

"Well, you could sell ice to an Eskimo, so well done."

She beams for a second then appears to stop herself, putting a pin in her happiness at the praise. Oh, that's not good. She's been hurt. I instantly think of Corey—what kind of name is *Corey,* anyway?—and how much I already want to maim him, but I have a feeling this is not a boy problem. She seems too self-contained for that.

"Okay, let's see. Do you want to ask me one?" I say. I don't want to put her on the spot first.

"Sure. Where did we meet?" she says, sitting on a side chair —the one farthest from the glass wall that looks onto the bedroom. Neither of us are even looking at that bed. Not when the other might catch it, anyway.

"Oh, that's easy. Isn't a day that goes by when I don't think of that."

"Excellent improv!" She puts the papers on her lap and applauds.

I grin. This is *fun.*

"We were at the lap pool at Freshwater Beach. When I looked up for a breath there you were, in stride with me, right alongside. I nearly drowned."

She throws her head back and laughs. Her hair swings. "Should I be scared that you're so good at this?"

"No. I'm a pro. I'm good at whatever I set my mind to. I get what I want." I am not mincing words. Why should I? There is something between us. And though I will do everything I can to keep this professional, I'm not going to be dishonest with her. I don't think I'm capable. The idea of lying to her strikes me as akin to strangling a fluffy kitten: unthinkable.

In a certain light, my overstating Dad's pressure on this

getting my act together thing could be looked at as less than upfront. But I tell myself that where the pressure originates is just a tiny detail.

"And what did you think of me when we first met that day?" This is a detail that isn't typed up. It's the kind of thing that requires personal interpretation to strike the right note.

She studies me. I enjoy the attention. "I thought, wow, she looks incredible in that bikini."

Now Olivia screws up her eyes.

I shrug. "What? Who's going to argue with that?"

"Well, I can rock a bikini." Lip tug. Oh, she's killing me.

"See? I knew it." It isn't easy to tear my gaze away and look back at the paper.

"And where did we go on our first date?" I ask her.

"10 William Street. Ooooh, the hot pretzels in the whipped bottarga dip. Yum." She flutters her eyes closed in pleasure and I'm reminded of her buffalo wing feast on the night we actually did meet.

There's a throbbing in my pants. "You love your food, don't you?"

"Well, I usually eat healthy. But I'm a big fan of the eighty-twenty rule. And when I go for my twenty, *boy,* do I make it count." Her eyes shoot up dramatically. She's got a presence you can't ignore. She shines.

"I remember, you enjoyed that dip so much you dragged your finger through the plate and licked the dregs off your finger." Oh, I shouldn't have gone there, my cock responds with a deep throb. "You shone so brightly when you did that. It's why I fell for you."

God, I can already see how truth and fantasy are tangling up out of control. I can't wholly wrap my head around my new motivations for this charade—they're nothing like the ones I would have had with Sheri in this role. It's a barrage of feelings that are new to me, and that could scare the ever-loving hell out of me if I let them, but I tell myself that the fact that those motivations brought me here, to this place with her, is all I need to know at the moment.

She lasers me with her gaze. I should take it slower. *Too late.* It's all gone serious suddenly. She inspects—I feel her eyes flit to my jaw, my mouth, back up to my eyes. Then she smiles; already I can distinguish this smile as genuine. I count—one, two, three—yup, there are her fingers at her lip.

"Ad-libbing. You're very good at it," she says, shaking her head in a way that doesn't match what she's saying.

"What about me? What would you say if someone asked what drew you to me?" I ask, my body leaning in, my legs opening wider.

She fidgets with her hair then straightens her posture. "Just look at you," she says. "Who would ask me that?"

"Well, there are plenty of girls who feel that way, but that's not the kind of girl *I'm* going to fall for, is it?"

She looks at her sheet. "You didn't put that in your report."

"You're the one who told me it's all about interpretation. Wasn't that what your cover letter was all about?"

"Not sure *this* is the job I was applying for."

"Do you want out?"

Olivia doesn't hesitate. And I hope that means we're on the same page with the honesty of our feelings; it seems vital amidst so much stagecraft. "No. No, I don't. I appreciate your help with my *situation.* Honestly, I've been feeling more hopeful since Friday night."

I can't help but smile. *I* made her more hopeful. Well, that's a start. And the fact that she can admit that so openly, shows that she was in a vulnerable place, well, that is completely new. And it makes me want to wrap her in my arms and never let her go.

What the fuck? Why should a woman like Olivia ever feel less than the megawattage she gives to the world?

She continues. "And I'm glad to help with yours in return. It's a good deal. And besides, I'm *enjoying* it."

More honesty. How can a situation like this instill so much of it? Where are the games, the bravado, the pretending not to be wowed by the money?

"Don't look so surprised. We hit it off right away."

"You mean wet shirt night?" If she's going to be so open, she deserves some frankness from me. I smile. I want to kiss her. It looks like she wants to kiss me too. But despite our sincerity, we're both trying to prove something: that this is professional, whatever the hell that would mean in this situation. I flip the script. "So, you've been to 10 William Street? I mean, outside of our date." I smirk.

"You bet your ass I've been there. I have my own seat. Don't even have to order. They know exactly what I want."

I can just picture her there. The best seat is the one at the back of the bar; it's got a bit more space and you can see the whole restaurant, as well as the chefs doing their thing. I know without a doubt that's her seat. She sits there enjoying a Keith Dolan song on the sound system. She logged on her sheet that *Knocked Me to My Knees* is her favorite song. *I could listen to him all day, every day,* she wrote.

"We should go one day," she says.

"What do you mean? We go all the time. We had our first date there. So, we go every Friday night when we're in town."

Again, with the giant, glowing smile. She's perfect.

We go through our living arrangement: she's about to officially move in with me, though she spends most of her time there anyway. The last topic covers the details of her parents. Judy and Rex are happily married after twenty-seven years. They live in a rural part of Connecticut, full of lush hills and apple orchards. "It's the kind of place people visit as they drive up to watch the leaves change in autumn."

I can't help but picture Olivia glowing in the rust tones of a fall sunset, in denim and flannel, as she described her look in the spreadsheet, listening to The Cure and Nine Inch Nails.

With palm flourishes and poetic landscape description, I picture her as she describes those long bike rides through the hilly terrain she detailed, Judy and Rex on the porch swing with cold lemonade when she returns. In that moment, I know I want to see this, feel it all with her, my arm over her shoulders, pulling her close while Rex and I watch the kielbasa she listed as his barbecue specialty sizzle over the coals. I never wanted a thing more.

The more I learn, the more I want her. And am I nuts, or does she feel the same?

"Next time we go to Braidwood, I want to take that bike ride with you," I say.

Her eyes squint even as she takes a sharp intake of breath. "Of course," she says, as she consciously tries to straighten her brow. Her legs cross, then re-cross the other way.

"If you go through the apple orchards when the wind's right, you can smell that crisp sweetness, feel it all through you." She closes her eyes, like she's remembering. It's an incredible thing to watch, the way her lips curl, her shoulders rise and fall. And when her eyes open again, she's softened to this disorienting weaving we're doing. She slides toward me, to the edge of her chair, then seems to catch herself. But she doesn't scoot back, just sits straighter. Then shakes her head and smiles at me.

"I know," I say, reaching for her hand. "I want that too."

Our faces are close, they seem to have homed in on each other without our realizing. "Kissing you in that place is my idea of heaven."

Her chest shudders, she shrinks back slightly.

"Don't be afraid," I say. "I won't let anything happen to you."

She smiles, her eyes grateful, like a weight has been lifted. Of course, it has, she's been so worried about everyone else. Hasn't let herself enjoy this kind of comfort in ages. But that's over now.

"Unless you want it to," I say. Our lips are so close. I can't help but stare at hers. I want to claim them, make them mine and no one else's. The space between us is closing. My body is in flames. Arousal is all. I dart my tongue out. She gasps. And this jars me back to reality. It's too much, too soon. I can't overwhelm her with all I'm feeling. I pull back, but at the same moment she goes to touch her lips to mine.

Immediately, her features freeze over. I've hurt her. Oh fuck. It's the last thing I wanted to do. But this is why we must wait. There are raw needs and wants and feelings flying around like mad. We need to tame this. Surely there's a way. Even as I think the words, I know they're pure rubbish. This will not be tamed.

The flames will only be stoked hotter—anger, anticipation, curiosity, intimacy—it's all combustible now. There's no stopping things once we've thrown in the match. It's just a matter of controlling the burn, but even that, when I see the hurt in her eyes at what she must see as my rejection, seems like a goal too lofty to achieve.

It's the right thing, I tell myself. But all I want to do is overtake her, kiss her everywhere, so hard that all the pain is gone and there's nothing but us.

Instead, she stands, trying to put a safer distance between us. There's a faux coldness to her voice, and it doesn't sit right. "I should probably get ready for dinner. I think we've got this attraction act down," she says. "I nearly got carried away there." She smiles like that answers everything, buttons it up neatly so we're both perfectly clear, when the truth is we're anything but.

I grab her hand to try to soothe the seas swirling inside her. But she gives me one quick squeeze then uncurls my fingers. Seeing the back of her feels like a warning. *Don't fuck this up.*

TEN

OLIVIA

I'm not going to lie, knowing he's naked in the steamy shower in the bathroom next to mine while I'm naked in my own steamy shower does cause an intense reaction in me. I'm only human. Every swipe of soap on my skin adds to my arousal.

I'm thrumming, thinking of the grid of his chest muscles, the way his cock must look at full mast, free and hungry on my account. I can feel my wetness gather, and no matter how cold I turn the taps, the heat of my body will not subside.

My hot and heavy state is not helped by the fact that getting dressed with any modesty is off the table care of the zipper up the back of my dress that requires his help. He's instantly behind me, helping to prove what I feel—that he has been watching me.

His fingers expertly loop down under the guise of securing the zip pull. Do I like it? Holy hell, yes, I do. I'm zinging by the time I fasten my earrings and twist before the mirror to see how the updo and the long shoulder dusters come together with the red dress.

And Aiden? Well, he doesn't appear to be concerned with modesty. He came out of that bathroom in a cloud of steam, wearing only a towel wrapped around his waist. And what a waist it was. I thought for sure he'd slip his briefs on under the towel, but *no siree bob!* He dropped the towel to the chair alongside and I got a view of the full monty. In that moment, I was ruined for asses. This one was perfect. There seems no point in seeking out another.

Before I know it, all that tight, muscled perfection is wrapped in a charcoal pinstripe suit—again with a crisp white button up and no tie. But this time I know what's underneath. And experiencing his process of shaving, showering, and suiting up, following our two-hour conversation, has added an intimacy to things that I hadn't expected.

By the time he closes the door to our room behind us, and takes my hand in his, the whole thing feels so real, and I feel so close to him that I have to remind myself this is fake. That he had snubbed my kiss earlier is a reminder. Is it the rejection making me want him more? Are we all just gluttons for punishment?

"You are stunning," Aiden says as we wait for the *lift*, aka elevator.

"You're not so bad yourself," I say.

We share a moment, still holding hands, looking into each other's eyes. He has to be feeling it too.

I'm lost in the sensation, but somehow we make our way to the dining room, which is low lit and inviting with wild-looking native floral arrangements and a three-piece band setting the tone.

Their rhythmic music only enhances the vibe between us. While I sit next to him, his hand draped over my shoulder, our talk, his fingers on my back, his beautiful nakedness, the way he looked spraying that heavenly cologne on his neck, it all hangs between us. And it's lovely.

His dad can see it. I can tell from the way he keeps looking at Aiden's palm on my bare skin.

We've compiled the data, studied and interpreted it expertly. I repeat this line and yet it feels nothing like that. It feels natural and that is why I allow myself to lean into Aiden when his arm is once again across my shoulders after our starters. When I do so his fingers graze my arm, sending shockwaves all through me. *Where is the data for this?*

I could look. But the truth is the data only helps if you want it. So why don't I want it? I *should* want it. Aiden is a world-class ladies' man, and the last person I need to be growing feelings for. Men like Aiden are exactly what landed me in this ridiculous situation in the first place. I vowed never to let that happen again and I meant it. But I had never experienced anything like this.

So, what if you just enjoy yourself for once, Olivia? Well, there's the little matter of this man being my boss. There's a reason the world is bogged down in sayings about not getting involved there. Because it's a mess—and certainly not the type of mess a woman in my situation can afford.

Lose my job, lose my visa. Go home a failure. Not an option for this girl, who has put her parents through so much worry in her short life. Besides, I'd already gotten carried away and he snubbed my advance, so why does my body keep wanting to try again? Why is his body doing the opposite of snubbing? And why, although his father is sitting right across from us, does this feel like anything but a show for his benefit? It feels like the whole room could disappear into oblivion and we wouldn't even notice.

"Aiden says you're going to bring P.I.C. up to date on the cutting edge of marketing. Is that true?"

I have to remember how to speak. Aiden has been drawing

delicious circles on the back of my neck and I've lost myself in the sensation.

"Sir—"

"Call me Marc."

His smile is so expert, it's frightening. These are Aiden's genes, I remind myself.

"Well, Marc, sir—"

Everyone laughs. The mood is light. Enjoyable. The few others at the table are quiet, cautious, and this makes me think it's not always this way.

"There are so many niches available to target with advertising these days. It's just a matter of finding your tribe and giving them what they want. I helped to increase my previous company's profit by 200 percent while I was there."

"Now that's a number I can wrap my head around." Sir Marc laughs and holds up his glass. Again, the whiskey. It's striking, the similarities between these men, but it's also clear that Aiden is different around his father than I've seen him.

He's more measured, careful, but trying his darnedest to appear anything but. He's mostly got it down pat, and if I hadn't been alone with him before, I wouldn't have picked up on it.

You know him. That's just crazy talk. You've known him all of three days.

ELEVEN

AIDEN

There isn't a man in the world more difficult to impress than my father. He's had too many pretty women, too much success, and too many proposals.

And yet, in walks Olivia—*not even trying to impress him. She's just being herself, the same self I saw before*—and her authenticity knocks him out, same way it did to me.

"Tell us about growing up in America," he says to her, over a rock lobster the size of a small child. From this angle, the boat-load of lies Dad and I have cobbled together in place of an actual relationship looks asinine. And yet, this is how we've managed to get by year after year.

I know how Dad sees me and pretends not to care and vice versa. Our relationship isn't the warm fuzzy kind where we work out the intricacies of how the other is feeling, where we stand together and collaborate on how we can make things right in a time of stress.

Instead, we stand far enough apart that a body language expert would have a field day. We politely and quietly don't get each other, but still, despite the ugly things he did to our family and the disdain he has for me for appearing to follow in his footsteps, we have our own undeniable connection that defies logic. I believe some people call this love, but this isn't a word uttered in my family. It's something you might, potentially observe under an expensive light for a moment, but you can never be quite sure. What I can be sure of, however, is that his respect is as vital as air or water to me, whether I want it to be or not.

I wonder which part of her childhood Olivia will choose to share. Her dossier was factual, not emotional like our conversation earlier, and I find myself feeling covetous of the scene she shared with me—her bicycle rides, the burnt leaves crinkling beneath the tires.

But it's obvious from spending a few of the liveliest minutes of my life with her that something doesn't add up between the lines of data and the feelings she can instigate with a glance. She runs deep, this incredible woman whose majestic smile seems capable of things years of my misguided efforts haven't achieved. I'm keen to see what she says.

"I'm from Connecticut. About halfway between Manhattan and Boston. It was the kind of simple, quaint place you picture when you hear *New England*—white church spires and picturesque bridges, leaves changing while we all hang maize on the doorways and pick our pumpkins." Her cheek apples are perfect, and I want to reach out and kiss one when she smiles at the memory.

Why don't you? Yes, why *don't* I? I brush my fingertips there and she turns to me. So does my father and everyone else at the table. I am not immune to her charms. I want to know her. I want her to know me. And the possession of this kind of knowledge feels completely different from any kind of personal knowledge I've experienced before. Each memory, each exchange, each new expression and lip tug is a strut in a bridge that brings us closer. I never considered this level of intimacy. Never knew it existed.

My father turns back to her. "And your parents?"

She sighs hugely, her eyelids fluttering. "I have the best parents in the world. Sacrificed everything for me. Never once mentioned it. Wouldn't have it any other way." She means every word. There's no doubt of that. My father is too polite to pry, and I'm glad. I don't want her talking about whatever she's holding back in front of him for the first time.

"Will we be meeting them?" he asks instead.

She looks to me. I take this one. Olivia reaches for her whiskey. "They're coming next month. Dying to see this dashing Aussie their daughter's fallen for."

Bless her, Olivia chokes on her sip.

But everyone laughs. This is what she does to people. And it's effortless. I meant to keep this professional, but in this moment, I doubt anyone could blame me if I flounder.

"We'll have to get them over to the family estate on the South Coast," my father continues. "They can see all the kangaroos they ever dreamed of. Aiden can take them surfing, and I'll grill them up a feast of steaks and sausages."

"No matter how much money he piles up, Dad always makes us suffer through his burnt steaks and sausages."

"Sounds perfect," Olivia says. But she tugs her lip. Of course, her parents won't be meeting mine. She'd never allow the farce to go that far, would she? It would be pure madness. Intellectually, I know that, and yet my heart says something quite different.

Obviously, when the time comes, we'll tell Dad we can't make it. I would tell myself he didn't really mean the invitation anyway, but I know that's not true. Olivia's worked her magic on him. Nothing makes sense, and it's a welcome feeling.

Finally, I make our excuses and walk Olivia out of the dining room. "Shall we go for a walk?" I ask. The grounds are incredible, and the night is clear and warm. And most importantly, I don't want the evening to end.

"Sure," she says, raising a shoulder. Her cheeks are pinked from a mix of whiskey and the way our bodies have been connected all night.

We make our way down the bougainvillea-lined path out to the rows of vines.

"Your dad isn't as scary as you made him out to be," she says.

"No, no. He *is*, but not with you. He likes you."

"Oh, stop. You don't have to flatter me. I've already agreed to your deal."

I stop, reach out for her arm. "I'm not flattering you. It's true. He isn't immune to your powers. No one is." I lock my eyes onto hers so she knows I'm serious.

She goes to grab for her lip, and I place my hand gently on hers to stop her.

She smiles. *You know me*, that smile says. *Yes, I do.* I hope my gaze, my touch, assures her of this, makes up for the stupid way I'd reacted to her kiss in the room earlier.

So why, suddenly, do I pull away, let my hand drop from her arm? Because she can't be this perfect, right? Something has to be wrong here.

At the edge of the garden, we approach the rows of grapes on the vines. The smell is incredible. It's all around us.

"How are we getting out of what your dad said, about my parents coming to your family estate?" she asks, stopping to pull off her heels, which she holds by the straps in one hand.

"We'll make our excuses. Obviously, that would be a disaster." *Then why are you picturing it? Everyone around the giant stone table on the verandah, laughing over Dad's chargrilled sausages? Your arm slung over her waist, holding her as close as humanly possible?*

"Obviously," she says. She flutters her lips in a long exhale.

"What have we gotten ourselves into?" she asks. We take our time along the first row in silence.

We're rounding the edge of the row and weaving back along the next one in the direction we just came from. "We're solving two problems. And we're doing a great job." Even I can see that my words are hollow. This isn't what she's talking about, and I know it.

Why does it feel so complicated all of a sudden? When we were practicing our lines, then acting them out, and genuinely enjoying ourselves at dinner, it was so simple—everything made sense, despite how ridiculously wacked the plan is. But now, here, alone with her, and all these conflicting feelings bobbing up, I feel lost and doing what I do in that situation: closing myself off.

But she doesn't seem to be handling the confusion in the same way. Of course, she wouldn't—she's the perfect mix of warmth, openness, and logic. She knows putting blinders on isn't going to solve anything. *But what if you're wrong about her? What if you've fallen for an incredible act? Rubbish! You sure?* I know what this about face is. It's disbelief and fear. *But you certainly won't admit that will you?*

Olivia stops walking, and I double back to her. We're face to face in the moonlight and the vines. It's perfect and all I want to do is smother the hesitation creeping into my mind and kiss her. She's perfect, the stray hairs like a masterpiece. As if she can read my mind, she reaches for my cheek, her hand grazing back to my ear, my hair, the back of my neck.

She closes her eyes and moves her lips toward mine. I'm watching, my body reacting on its own accord. I feel my cock twitch, my feet step closer.

But just as our lips are about to touch, I pull back and when she should be making contact, there's nothing but air. Her eyes flash open and she's looking at me with raw hurt and anger. How on God's earth have I done this again?

You, my friend, have just proven you are afraid.

Fuck no.

Then what the hell was that?

I know this autopilot mode of mine. Didn't expect it to come up with Olivia, though. My face is not unkind, but any emotion is miles beneath the surface, safe and sound. "All of a sudden, I'm a bit tired," I say, hating myself.

"Like hell you are," she says, arching a brow.

I am not used to being challenged. "Are you calling me a liar?"

"Yes. Yes, I am. You, Aiden Wheatley, are lying. And I think it's because you're scared."

I laugh. "That's absurd." *It so isn't.*

She shakes her head. "You want to keep this professional? Well, I'll keep it as professional as you can imagine," she says.

I don't know what she has in mind, but I know I'm not going to like it. And I wish more than anything I could rewind and not have said those words, and instead, kissed her the way I wanted to. I wish I were kissing her still, holding her in my arms the way I'm desperate to.

"That's good news. Excellent job tonight. Better than I could have hoped for."

OLIVIA

How a man with such presence and intelligence could take an evening from a perfect ten to a negative three in twenty seconds is beyond me. But Aiden manages it, snubbing me like that in the vineyard, *for the second time,* then changing the discourse so that all the personal connections we'd made were scrubbed clean.

I'm fuming as I find myself in my private bathroom back in our suite. I have a plan, though. I'm going to make him feel as stupid as he made me feel when I leaned in for that kiss and he backed away. Because we all know two wrongs make a right. And Aiden seems to have a knack for bringing out that mature side of me. In fact, he only brings out extremes, which frightens the bejesus out of me, considering how I landed Down Under in the first place.

What I need to do is get myself stuck into the data, so I can see what's what and create a course of action based on evidence.

The data from this evening:

1. We shared a few moments rehearsing; we were about to share a kiss in the suite when Aiden suddenly froze up.
2. We shared a few moments during dinner.
3. We were about to share a kiss in the vineyard when Aiden suddenly froze up.
4. When that happened, he immediately retreated to language about keeping it professional.

SO, what can I learn here? When everything was going according to plan, he was easy, relaxed, fun, and intimate. His guard was down. But the second we went off script to put feelings into action, he pulled back. Twice. A small data set, but a pattern all the same.

And he's right. Us being together is a bad idea. For all sorts of reasons—the largest of which is that he's my boss.

But that's not going to stop me from showing him I've got his number. And giving him a little of his own medicine.

I smile at my reflection in the mirror because I've pulled out all the stops. It's a bit unfair. I've slipped on a very tiny nighty. It's milky pink silk and black lace and doesn't leave much to the imagination. My nipples are on full display beneath the flimsy fabric, and if I lean over, he'll get the full picture of my breasts.

When I emerge into the room, he's on the sofa with a whiskey, tapping at his laptop. There's another whiskey sweating in a glass on the table beside him.

He looks up when he sees me coming and tries to act like this getup has no effect on him. But his eyes and lips quirk and I know I've got him.

I sit down and cross my legs alongside him. I know my nightie is riding up. I see him notice.

He hands me the glass.

"Thanks," I say. "Just one and I'm gonna hit the hay. I am *beat*." I take a nice, warming sip, then lick my lips.

"You look incredible," he says.

"This old thing?" I say. "It's just so hot, I can barely stand to wear anything to bed."

"Well, don't let me stand in your way," he says.

I nearly break character by laughing. But I won't let him get off that easily.

"I should be okay in this," I say, looking down at my body, and in doing so, inviting him to do the same.

"Depends on your definition of okay."

I take another sip. I don't even know the words are going to come out of my mouth, but the second they do, I know they're perfect for getting back at him. What man could resist such a challenge? "I just want to make sure you know that we are not going to have sex. There's chemistry between us, sure. But getting emotionally involved is just going to complicate things. Like you said, we need to keep it professional."

"Which is why you wore that very professional outfit," he says.

"This is the kind of thing your girlfriend would be wearing, isn't it? We need to be authentic."

Thankfully, he spares me the argument that nobody's watching now.

Instead, he nods.

"Well, I think I'll call it a night," I say, standing, reaching around to the back of my neck to loosen some of the tension, understanding the effect this will have on him.

"Do you need some help with that?" he asks.

"That would be great," I say. He's playing right into my hand. I'll get him all worked up then leave him flat. Then we'll be even. Two totally mature adults.

He turns sideways then pats the space between us on the couch.

I scooch over slightly. Aiden closes the space by sliding even nearer. Oh, I hadn't counted on him smelling this good. I swallow, trying to keep it quiet.

I'm wide-eyed, and now I feel exposed because he can see how tense every bit of my back is stacked in its perfect line.

I can feel him shifting, spreading his legs and sliding the one at the back of the couch out straight, so it's between me and the cushions. When it settles in a position where our legs are touching, a wave of reaction washes over me. I try to conceal it, but I can feel my knee tremble.

He places two gentle palms over my shoulders and that scent of him—bright, vibrant, masculine—compounds. The combination of the leg touching, the smell, my obvious tension, and his hands on my shoulders are too much. I can't breathe. I have to open my mouth wide to take in any air at all.

His thumbs press in exactly the right spot. It's heaven.

"Ooooh." Before I know it, I'm making sex noises. *Great job, Olivia! You're really showing him.* I should get up right now and leave it at that.

"Ahhhh." But it feels too good. He works at the soreness and then begins to knead the area around the knots.

"See? You're in good hands." Why is every word that comes out of his mouth arousing? Is it his chiseled jaw, his aforementioned expert, large hands? The sexy, casual confidence of the Australian accent? Probably all the above.

I begin to relax into the feel of his fingers and palms, applying pressure and rhythm in all the right places.

"So, what's got you so tense?" And then he says that.

You. "Nothing. I don't like lying. That's all."

"I don't either. It's funny though. When we were down there, it didn't feel like lying. It felt great."

So, he felt it too. Or is this just part of making it all work, building me up so I'll give my best performance? That thought is too ugly. In fact, the second it presents itself, I know it isn't true. It doesn't jive with anything about him.

In my heart, even in the spaces between my neatly numbered list of facts, I know everything I thought earlier is true. He's *scared.* And that I can understand. I can also understand keeping it to himself. And yet, it still stings. *Because you're looking at yourself in the mirror.*

"It was fun," I agree. *Who's being petulant now?*

His fingers freeze and I hear his lips pop. I picture the small circle of space between them and ache to turn around.

He returns to the massage without a word.

Our words aren't working. Because we aren't being honest.

And I'm meant to be teasing him. Only, Aiden rubbing my skin is exquisite and seems to be saying all the things I'm unable to.

He gently works his way up, his hands feathering my neck, then rubbing, sweeping my hair aside, as I bend one way and then other to give him better access.

His fingers knead and I close my eyes, enjoying the sensations. The touch becomes less therapeutic and more erotic, his fingers sliding down my spine, then back up and out, along my arm, to the inside of my wrist, then up to the tender skin behind my ear.

He shifts. And now I feel the whisper of his breath there. It's at a distance, and yet close enough. I let my head fall back in pleasure and that's when I feel his lips make contact with my neck. I shiver. And that's too revealing.

Suddenly, I spring to my feet, avoid his eyes, unable to avoid the hard cock I'd sensed behind me, and shake my head out. "Thanks. That was a big help. I'm going to bed now."

He sees me see that throbbing thing between us, the one that will change everything. His eyes are smiling as I turn to go. He's watching me, and I leave him high and dry. But I'm not sure that's a win.

The night wears on, and he fails to sleep on the floor alongside me. I'm alone in the bed and find myself in the same predicament, the desire in the room is palpable, suffocating in its rising pressure. Every time I move, I feel like I'm on fire. Each time I see his muscles ripple, I think I might explode.

It's a *very* long night.

TWELVE

AIDEN

I have never seen someone lie so completely still when it's so obvious they aren't sleeping. This is a woman who does not want to show an ounce of weakness. The whole *look at my sexy negligee, but you can't touch* show backfired.

She was getting so hot and heavy as I massaged her, I could feel her go liquid under my fingertips. We should have been sharing a night of passion and instead, we spent the night randy as fuck with no satisfaction in sight. *Everybody wins!*

What happened to that open woman I kissed that first night walking her home from the Old Grand Hotel in my sopping wet shirt? *You pissed her off by showing her your true feelings, then pulling the shades down.* But now we're both playing a little game, and the competition is helping to take the edge off the blue balls. It's a way of acting out in place of devouring each other, which is what we clearly want to do. Just like in the schoolyard all those years ago. It's good to see I've matured.

I should put it out there, pull her into my arms and tell her to forget this silly game we're playing. But I can't. She's too—too *everything*. And the game is revealing bits of her I don't think she would have chosen to show me. Like what makes her so loathe to show any weakness.

There's a chink in her armor. I just have to work out what it is. And I have a plan to bring her back to that close place we were sharing until I screwed it up. It's a fucking good one too. When she dozes off, I text the directive.

THIRTEEN

OLIVIA

The breakout room where my department is meeting up with one of the speaker's disciples is of the same early-settler style of the rest of the property. It's full of dark wood, high archways, and stone and plaster detail. You can smell the history and I can feel my fingers itching to Google the way life was when this place was built. People think facts are boring, but they flesh everything out. We'd be nothing without them. Nothing you could trust, anyway.

We're here to put into action the five-step method to more efficient time management that everyone is so hyped up about after the lecture. I'm the first one in my brand-new department —I'll have an assistant who's meant to start next week—and so it's Poppy's group I'm in here with. Despite the structure, I'm meant to be working independently on this planning since they have no idea what it is I do.

Poppy still finds the need to sneer at me when she sees me enter the room. I see her turn to the older woman at her side, the one who always hands out chocolates to everyone on Thursdays, and whisper something in her ear. The usually kind, generous woman glares at me and she shakes her head.

Wonderful. Poppy's spreading lies about me. I slept my way into my salary. Just what I need. *If there are going to be rumors, you might as well be putting some substance to them.* That's just my stretched-to-the-limit libido talking. Aiden tortured me right back last night and we were both riding the edge of desperation through to sunrise. Let's face it, there were no winners.

Quite the opposite, I woke this morning feeling sheepish. My behavior was childish. I can't explain why Aiden brings this out in me, but I know the sensations I've been experiencing are new to me, so it's no wonder my behavior follows suit. Why can't I get a handle on it? Well, I don't have an answer to that.

Even now, the image of Aiden's taut, thick arms, looking irresistible crossed behind his head atop the down pillow on the floor turns my core molten. This gets me conjuring the picture-perfect planes of his bare chest. He had the blanket slung unbelievably low—like a fig leaf in a Renaissance painting—and I couldn't help but think he was trying to give me a shot of my own medicine.

And oh, brother, did it work. That V with its whisper of hair trailing down to the glorious cock was outlined in full relief by the thin blanket. The image is branded in my brain as Poppy whispers her poison.

Now the motivation for my putting him off is murky. What last night had felt like sass and strength now smacks of obviousness and more than a dash of immaturity. Also, wouldn't it have been more fun to run my hands up and down the sculptured muscles of that chest, trace my fingers down that victory V, slip my pinky over the crown I kept stealing glances at, wrap my fist around the length of him?

Sure. More fun, but more dangerous, too, I remind myself. *You're playing with fire.* You're feeling incredibly close to him because of the charade you're putting on—knowing more about each other than you ever would at this stage, or perhaps any stage, and the intimate bubble of truth the two of you share is only heightening that feeling of intimacy. Everything has an explanation if you look at the facts. Which is much easier to do without that movie-star chest in my face. I giggle. Out loud.

Poppy turns.

Look at me getting myself in trouble anyway. *Another argument for feeling the victory V.* As if I needed another one, my next thought is that I wish Aiden were here to witness Poppy's behavior. I'm positive more than anything that he would not stand for it. *There you go, drawing a ring around the two of you, like a team, a daring duo, a* couple.

No. Another argument for *not* giving into temptation, more like. You want to be in Australia, and more than anything, you need to show your parents you are happy and stable and healthy. They don't need another reason to worry about their sickly little girl.

The speaker is quite good. He's been drinking his boss's multi-billion-dollar *New York Times* Best-Selling Kool-Aid, sure, but it's backed up by facts, comes with an app that is incredibly user-friendly and well thought-out, and makes me look at my immediate, short-term, medium-term, and long-term goals in a way that even outdoes my own impeccable system.

This company is world-class. I am lucky to be here. Another argument—along with my distraction—for not giving into temptation.

Of course, I'm working on my own while Poppy and her team are giggling and high on the collective energy of this efficiency master.

I'm admiring the color-coding system and wondering about the back-end code, something I have a passion for, when I hear my name whisper-screamed and see everyone look up.

I'm strong. I have looked death in the face more times than I can recall. The Poppys of this world are no match for my strength. I will not look up, will let the glares remain at the periphery of my vision, and not give a shit about what they say. I'm no stranger to this kind of treatment.

Sure, I've spent most of my life in and out of hospitals, but I'm pretty, so people think everything comes easy to me, which automatically makes them hate me, and assume I'm dumb. My mother used to say that my beauty was nature's way of making us smile through the horrors of the tubes and the eye patch and the sleepless nights, watching me first in the protective bassinet of the NICU, and then in the children's wards with all the kids playing games like we weren't at death's door.

"Your liquid green eyes are like a soothing river, your perfect smile a balm. I stared and stared at them," she told me, most recently when we had a teary phone conversation about how happy she was for me, and how she couldn't wait for her trip to see my beautiful new life in person.

Only I had tears streaming down my face for a different reason. It had only been a week since I caught Corey mounting that pixie-haired slut in my bed. And I couldn't bring myself to put Mom through any more pain.

My life is a gift. She's told me that so many times. And here I am, making a complete mess of it because I'd run headfirst into my first delirious taste of love—maybe not love so much as freedom, I'm beginning to see, but the mess has been made all the same.

Oh, I had the facts. Corey was a shameless flirt amongst other irresponsible behaviors I was able to chalk up to a handsome Aussie enjoying himself overseas. But I couldn't bring myself to face them in their true light. I didn't want to. Because when had life been so sweet and pleasurable and *unplanned* before? Never.

For obvious reasons, I'd sworn off such behavior before. But, dipped in the candy of Corey's recklessness, it's irresistible to someone as measured as me. A whole new world. Every day a new adventure.

I should have known better. But this time, I will. So what if Aiden and I shared a couple of ridiculously intense kisses that made me forget my name? So what if his hand wrapped around my shoulder made my body pulse with desire? These were not facts. These were the kinds of things that brought a person to part with their logic. I had the proof to back that up.

But there had to be a middle ground between those two, certainly, a place where life could be delicious and surprising, unfolding before you like a present, but also something stable you could count on.

If I could face all that, I can certainly face a jealous cow like Poppy, who hates me because of my salary, and if my mom is right, my beauty, to which she likely attributes my success and aforementioned salary. It isn't true, but I'm certainly not in a position to argue, given I'm meant to be in a serious relationship with Aiden. I'd hate me too.

I put my head down and concentrate on my goals. They are all work related in this setting, obviously. But seeing them all there makes me realize how strange it all looks without anything having to do with love, a life with someone.

And when I picture that someone, there's Mr. Wet Shirt Fig Leaf, threatening to part me and my senses once again.

FOURTEEN

AIDEN

O n the second afternoon of the conference, there's none of the leisure time to huddle up in our suite and get to know each other under the pretense of perfecting our farce. It's a bit of a shame because that was immensely enjoyable.

Dare I say even last night's sweet torture was a kind of exquisite pleasure, full and ripe with the tensions between us. Sure, we both had our reasons for not giving in, but we both knew we would eventually. It's something as certain as the sun's ascent tomorrow.

Instead, it's two ships passing in the early night, getting ready for tonight's dinner and entertainment, which was changed at the last minute (last night after my text), for Olivia's pleasure. Why did I go to the trouble? Because I screwed up when I didn't accept her kiss. I need to show her how much I care.

Keith Dolan is her all-time favorite. I always thought he was a little too sentimental, but listening to him on my run this morning, under the veil of Olivia's intense fandom, the words took on new meaning.

I was turning into a weenie, and yet, there I was on the

treadmill, grinning from ear to ear at the idea of how these words affected her, and how they were saying the kinds of things I felt for her and meant to show her.

I'm tempted to put Dolan's latest release on Spotify for her right now as she fastens a cuff of gold around her wrist, but that would be too much of a give. Instead, I put on some music I love to see *her* reaction to. *And you care what it is, don't you? You want her to love it.* I do. I really do.

I understand this is an old Australian band and she probably doesn't know the song, but I want to see her listen to it, hopefully for the first time. I want to be the one to show it to her, to watch the lyrics work their way into her soul.

She's glamorous in snow white, the neckline cut on a diagonal so one shoulder is bare. The dress is sculptured, like something a Bond girl would wear, and she rocks it. Tonight, her hair's down in Hollywood waves alongside her eye. Stunning.

I was waiting for her to ask me to zip her up again, but apparently this one doesn't have a zip. If I wasn't enjoying the view so much, I'd be utterly disappointed.

I tap PLAY as she's fastening a knot of gold onto her earlobe. Her eyes are at the ceiling. There's consideration at her brow. Then a softening of her features and posture, like the music is washing over her.

If possible, she looks even more stunning this way. She closes her eyes and listens, her head bobbing slowly to the beat. It's an intense song, deep want and longing at its core. She smiles at the line "You, there's only you." Then seems to catch herself, shakes her head and smiles, looking my way.

"I like that song. Who's it by?"

I tell her the name of the band and watch as she taps it into her playlist.

We stand there, listening to it in silence, which is somehow more intimate than the talking felt. We're wrapped in the music, and as it ends, the atmosphere it creates doesn't dissipate. It follows us out the door and to the dining room. At the elevator, Olivia again allows herself to move closer to me. Is she getting into character? Or is she finished with the quid pro quo of last night?

People are complicated, and she's inside my arm, whatever the reason. So, I'm just going to be happy that she's let her guard down for me again. And I know she's going to be so happy when she sees this evening's entertainment, that I hope this not only fixes things between us but helps take it to the next level.

Dad's looking pompous as always in his pricey suit and RM Williams, which he thinks make him look like a down-to-earth bloke. They do not. The way he looks at me with Olivia is so different than his usual take on me that I kind of want to punch him. But at the same time, I get it. She makes me better. She'd make anyone better. It's crazy to think how I wound up here with her.

The dinner's just as incredible—a starter of Tasmanian smoked salmon gravlax, the best steak I've ever had for a main course, and then a melty-centered chocolate cake for dessert that makes Olivia moan in a way that I'm not the only one to notice.

Before I know it, the white-gloved staff are clearing away the last of the plates and topping up the whiskeys.

"So, who's this mystery singer you've got for us tonight, Aiden?" Dad asks.

Olivia sits up straight. "Yes! Please tell us. I've been hearing people whisper about it all day."

"Who do they think it is?"

"I heard Elton John in the ladies' room before."

There are gales of laughter. "I'm afraid Sir Elton was otherwise booked for the evening," I say.

Marc Wheatley is flanked by his assistant and the C.F.O.,

Christopher Adams, who's been with the company since it was one room in a graffitied mini mall. Both seem to keep their conversation mostly with their boss, but it's clear they don't miss a beat.

"Well, I can tell you who we *had* before Aiden had us make a very expensive last-minute change," the assistant, Ed, says.

Everyone leans in.

"Katy Perry."

"Shut up!" That's Olivia.

Again, laughter. It's something in her delivery, the softening around her eyes that disarms everyone, I think. But then I'm unsure, there are so many glowing parts to her that it could be any one of them. It's the essence of *je ne sais quoi*. It's a mysterious Olivia-ness you can't pin down. *You should stop trying to.*

When her lashes close in a heart-skipping beat, the famous butterfly metaphor springs to mind, and I wonder what else in the world is being set off by the delicate flutter of her lashes at this table. That thought leads to another: all of this specialness is of this particular moment in time. It won't last. It can't. Another vote for keeping it professional.

But there are times when the heart wins out over the head, no matter the strength of the rationale. And both my heart and my head know who's won. They've known from the moment I laid eyes on her.

She's going to be so thrilled when she sees Keith Dolan. My chest actually flutters with anticipation. Still, it feels incredible to be so swept away. So what if it's a bit girly? I sure as fuck won't tell anyone.

"Oh, this is gonna be amazing, if you kicked out Katy Perry for them. Katy-effing-Perry," this from my father's righthand man, Christopher, who only knows Katy Perry because he knows wealth and success.

I don't think Ed, on the other hand, will ever forgive me,

because he's a die-hard Katy Perry fan, which is why I didn't have him make the arrangements to change the talent for Olivia's benefit. He probably would have arranged to have Dolan poisoned so we'd have to stick with the original plan.

As it is, he looks like a boy whose puppy just died. All's fair in love and war, but I already paid Katy double for next year, plus her cancellation fee for today. Hopefully Ed will forgive me.

A light flashes on the stage and a hush runs across the room. Olivia's gaze flicks my way and the butterflies go mad, all trying to escape at once, it feels like.

A gorgeous woman dressed in head-to-toe black leather slinks onto the stage and stops at the microphone under the spotlight. Her black hair glistens.

"Ladies and gentlemen," she says in a husky, British accent.

I turn to Olivia, so I won't miss one second of her reaction.

"Please put your hands together for the incredible Mr. Keith Dolan!"

The room stands in synchronicity and the applause is deafening, but I only see Olivia, who is in shock. Her glistening eyes, lined in black, bulge. I've never seen so much white in a pair of eyes. Instantly, she puts it together and her head suddenly swivels my way.

The fucking smile I get is worth every bit of effort, every penny. I would have paid double. Triple. It's as if Olivia has the ability to dig deeper, feel more, *give* more of that feeling than anyone on the planet. I don't know how she does it, but I want more.

I try not to show all of that at once, because I know it will overwhelm her the way it's overwhelming me—especially after the we're-just-being professional act we've been trying to maintain. But it's impossible. I am so purely happy. I see the happiness, with a twinge of overwhelm, yes, reflected in her eyes as I hear the applause increase to an ear-shattering volume, and Dolan's amped footsteps approach the mic.

She turns slowly from me, like she's tearing herself away, and that super-refined happiness bursts from every feature on Olivia's face.

Dolan is cool in denim and a white tee shirt. What was I thinking? She'll probably fall in love with him. *Is that jealousy? Oh, you know what that means. You've got it bad.*

He looks directly at our table, noticing Olivia, of course. You'd have to be blind not to, and he looks right at her as he starts playing the song she told me was her favorite. The first chord strum is the kind of deeply pained note that hits you right in the heart, obliterating all the walls you've erected. He's fucking good. Perhaps I'll be forgiven for booting Katy Perry after all.

"Yoouuu—" He lets the word go on and on. His eyes squeeze in feeling, and it's impossible not to be caught up in its net. "—never loved me." His eyes pop open. He *is* the pain. He's found a way to mainline it and wash it over everyone.

Olivia is clutching her dress at her chest and I can see her trembling like she's trying not to cry. I can only imagine the pain she's suffered if this is where she finds her solace. In the depth of her passion—to this *single line of a song*—it's clear she's experienced life in a way I wouldn't know the first thing about.

But I want in. And I want to be the one to bring that depth of passion to a place of pleasure and comfort, safety, and love. Because that is what she deserves.

Halfway through the show, I realize I'm not faking a fucking thing. And that this whole shenanigan we're trying to pull off is ludicrous. And still, the idea of coming clean about it is abso-fucking-lutely terrifying.

Do I deserve to be trusted with the happiness of this woman? She's in a whole other league, one I never even knew existed. How could I possibly give her what she needs? And given the way we met, what would ever make me believe that *she* would trust *me*?

I try to be subtle about gauging the vibe of my dad. His eyes are glued to Olivia. It's clear he believes our farce and probably wishes he'd found an Olivia of his own before he lost all desire for meaningful connection with a woman. I can't blame him for that.

It's an hour and forty-five minutes of heart-wrenching, testosterone-fueled raw emotion, and then the light goes out. From the dark stage, Dolan's Southern Texas cowboy accent says, "Come on up here, Olivia."

It takes her a second to register what he's said. As soon as she does, she shoots me a shocked, deeply warm look.

"I got a song to sing to you."

She stands and the room rips into applause. Her smile is so megawatt, it could burn the whole place down.

It's the other song she played for me. The one about being knocked to your knees by love. "It seems you've knocked someone to their knees."

Now the room stands for the applause. Everyone knows this tune. It was his first big hit. And there's a reason for that. It's the way each and every one of us on this earth is desperate to feel.

Olivia slowly makes her way to the stage, her heels sound-less as he starts the hypnotic guitar riff, which feels like being yanked uncontrollably along a current.

DROWNING and loving every minute of it.
Nothing will ever be like this.
It's—
Your light.
Let it blind me.

Don't stop.
Don't make me stop.

SHE'S STANDING inches from Keith Dolan up on the stage and yet she's staring at me the entire time. Every word is ours. There are tears streaming down her face and I can't help but get up there with her and wipe them with my finger. She's staring at me like we are exactly this to each other. And we are. Despite all the odds, the things unsaid, we are. I take her in my arms and kiss her, my lips saying all this.

Slowly, I let her plump lip go, and not even believing my actions myself, I descend to my knees, squeezing both of her hands in mine.

The crowd goes wild. I couldn't give a fuck about them, about my father, about any of it but her.

Dolan nods slowly.

We stand there, our stare built of unfiltered love, the rest of the song plays—it's all guitar, no words, just feeling, and it's the most perfect, honest moment of my life.

FIFTEEN

OLIVIA

I am overloaded on bliss. It's not a place I'm familiar with. Excepting the Corey moment of weakness, I pride myself on my measured approach to life. I have seen friends' relationships crash and burn around me, but I keep it even keeled and have, for the most part, managed to avoid such turmoil.

But I think I can say those days are officially behind me. Whatever I thought I might be onto with the idea of a middle ground is smashed and crunched underfoot. Keith Dolan singing his beautiful, striated lyrics to me, Aiden Wheatley on his knees, the way Keith is singing with such murderous passion for all the world to see. Holy Mother of God.

My logic has officially left the building. What did I ever want with boring old logic when I could have this sheer, rapturous bliss? It's the kind of feelings you sell your soul for. And if you've ever had this top-shelf quality of bliss, you see that you cannot wait to sign with your own blood on the dotted line. Whatever the consequences.

In this moment, our entire connection from the first moment to now is kaleidoscopic. I can see it all arranged to lead us to this moment and each tiny speck of it is brilliant. From this point of view, it seems I knew from the second Aiden sidled up to the bar stool alongside me that there was something *kismet* about us.

Otherwise, how could I have agreed to such a ridiculous scheme? Because let's be honest here in this moment, is this the kind of thing you do for your parents? If your parents were watching you, would they say, *yes, this is the perfect idea? What a wonderful choice you're making. The whole point is for us not to worry about you. It doesn't matter if we really should be, as long as you make us* think *you're fine, that's what really matters for us.*

The applause goes on for a long while, and it's deafening. And I don't think Keith has ever held a note longer, his eyes squeezed, his hands tight on the mic. But at some point, Keith takes his bow, the room clears out, and it's just Aiden and me.

He pulls me to sit next to him on the stage floor, our legs hanging over the edge. It's bright and the staff are stripping the table linens and upending chairs, and Aiden and I are just holding hands and gazing into each other's eyes. My heart is beating so fast, I'm sure he can see it.

I don't know how many hoops he had to jump through to get Keith Dolan here just for me, but I know it's symbolic. It's saying all those things that song said, and ridiculous as it is, I can feel the word dancing around in my head, daring me to put it out into the world: *love, love, love.*

"Come on," he says. His words are breathy, heavy, the way everything feels. His hand wrapped around mine ratchets everything up to a level where I'm not sure I can control myself.

We head up to our suite. It's been cleaned and everything looks staged for sex and that is not going to help the way I am feeling right now. The lights are low, there's soft music playing, and the bed's been turned down. Rose petals have been dropped on the comforter as if from heaven.

The second the door is closed behind us, Aiden pulls me to

him. "I'm so sorry about last night. I wanted to kiss you out in that vineyard more than I've ever wanted anything in my life. And it scared me."

"Well, you are the world's best apologizer. I almost want to pick another fight to see what you bring me next. *Keith. Dolan.* I still cannot believe it."

He sweeps a tendril behind my ear. I shiver. "Well, there was a moment there when I thought I was going to have to tell him to back off. But if I start down that road, I'd be doing that all the time. Everyone in that room fell in love with you tonight."

My chest thumps at the sound of the L word on his tongue. Is it banging around his head too?

I smile. And as I do, Aiden kisses the corner of my mouth. The feel of his lips on mine has been consuming me so deeply that the reality of it is almost too much. I melt a little under his touch.

"What are you doing to me, Olivia? That smile has a hold on me. I dreamed about it all night. Please let me show you how I feel."

I don't trust myself to speak. I dip my chin in agreement and part my lips as his caress mine. His tongue thrusts and I feel my body burn. He goes deeper and I pull the back of his head. I want more, all of him. He growls into my mouth and his hands encircle my back, dropping deliciously slowly toward my waist, where he pulls me to him.

His cock is straining, and I'm the one who pushes him hard against me. I wriggle and moan. This ramps things up. His tongue leaves my mouth and kisses, sucks, at my neck, my ear, my bare shoulder, his hands smoothing my hair, gripping it in his fingers. Then he's at my mouth again.

My eyes are closed in ecstasy. I don't know how long we are lapping and licking at each other this way, but I couldn't drag myself away if the room were burning down around us.

Then suddenly, he stops. He lifts me, hands beneath knees and back and carries me to the bed.

I was imagining this all last night when I was in my suggestive lingerie, but now that it's happening it's better than I could have imagined.

"I'm still not having sex with you," I say before I know I'm going to.

He throws his head back and laughs. "Obviously."

I smile then squint as he lowers me gently, so I'm standing against the foot of the bed. "I mean it," I say. Then I reach down and slide my dress up, slow as anything. I see his cock twitch and I smile. My spine tingles.

"You're not taking your clothes off either, right?"

"Exactly."

"And I'm not putting my mouth on your breast and licking your nipple." He reaches beneath my bra and cups my breast. My breath catches. His finger slips over my pebbled nipple, and it's so sensitive, I can't breathe. He goes in and sucks my nipple, then laps it up the way he just described as something he would not do. It's so hard and overloaded with sensation, I might explode.

"Let's get you more comfortable," Aiden says, then reaches around to unhook my bra.

I'm standing, bare, my shaved body in nothing but heels. I feel a pulse deep down as he lets the bra fall to the ground, then slides his hand down my breasts, grazes my sides, my hips.

"Better?" he asks.

"Too good," I say. "That's the problem."

"No such thing," he says, and yanks me close, his tongue thrusting into my mouth again. This time his hands cup my ass, pulling my slick opening apart, and I feel the muscles of my entrance beat for him. This is going to end so badly.

His touch is gone as soon as I feel it. He shrugs his way out of his jacket, frees his shirt from his pants, starts to unbuckle his belt. The way his fingers work his button and fly is magic. I watch his every move, waiting to see it. Then finally, his black briefs are in view, his impressive cock at full mast. He looks down and puts my hand there. His head falls back at just the touch of my fingers over the cotton.

I moan as I feel a shot of liquid run down my leg. Just from seeing him in his underwear. "This is not happening."

"Never."

"And if it was, it would be fake, like our relationship," I say. He freezes, his hand, which was again tangling in my hair loses its grip. Then he smiles, gets that I've stumbled upon something I can deal with.

"Nothing real about this," he says, lowering his boxer briefs to free his cock.

"Won't even remember your name in the morning," I say.

"Exactly, Athena."

I roar with laughter, with lust, with desire. Nothing will ever feel this good again.

And then we press into each other and my breath catches. Never mind, it's already better. He's not just pushing now, but overtaking me in the best possible way, claiming, the way deep down, I have always fantasized about. With his palm on my chest, he lowers me back on the bed, lies over me, pushing my hair away from my face. Our mouths crash again, and this time, the agreement made, it's urgent and raw, our desire finally given freedom to be out with it.

I feel his shaft rub at the lips of my pussy, and when he sees the way my back arches, I bite down on his tongue, he keeps at it. He's on my slick skin. I hear the wetness there. I want nothing more than to take him in. All it would take is a slight tilt of my hips and on the next trust, his tip would be at my opening. I can't. I won't.

Once more, he runs the length of himself against my cunt, up to his base, then back. We're playing a game of how far will we take this. I twitch to let him in but manage to hold back. My legs are quivering with the effort. Then he's working his cock down again and I can't stop myself from tilting so his tip is at my opening. His eyes lock onto mine. We freeze that way, at the edge of sanity, the edge of where we were safe, rational. Where are we about to go?

He swallows. There's nothing fake about this moment and we both know it. He rises and pulls me up too. I'm sitting and he's standing before me, bent over, his hands on my face, my body a tight knot of need. Then I watch his perfect silhouette as he goes to his bedside table and pulls a condom out of his drawer. The vision of him sliding it down his length is something I won't ever forget.

"I've got your back," he says. And thank God for that.

And then he's laying me gently down on the bed, and without another moment's hesitation, he slides inside as I tighten around him.

"Unreal," I whisper.

But it's developed into a different meaning now, and from the wolfish look in his eye, he knows it.

SIXTEEN

AIDEN

Madness. It's the only way I can come close to naming the way I feel, filling Olivia to the hilt, our eyes gazing deep into each other's souls like we've finally become whole. The most exquisite, elusive madness of love. I will never be the same again.

I'd like to tell myself I knew it would work out this way from the moment I marched up to her at the bar of the hotel, but I have never believed in this kind of thing. What evidence did I have of its existence? Other people claimed to have found it, but other people say a lot of ridiculous shit. I knew something was different that night, but I certainly didn't know it was *this* different.

I'm completely blown away by her. Every bit of her is screaming that she's mine, body and soul. I want nothing more than to make it official. I get an idea. And the idea that it could bring us even closer than we are in this moment is so erotic I start thrusting so deeply and suddenly I am so close to orgasm, my thighs are shaking.

"More," she says. "Give me more. More."

I know what she's doing. We're pretending it's not real, but this word is not mere dirty talk. It's real. She feels the way I do. She spreads her legs wider, bucks wildly. She's hugging so tightly around my cock. I'm so close. The edge is near. It's threatening to overtake me.

"Give me everything," she says. Olivia spasms, twitches around me. I call her name, then I'm over the edge, falling. "I'm coming," I say. I'm almost yelling, like it's an unbelievable thing the way I feel.

She clutches me closer inside her as I let go, crossing into the abyss. I look into her eyes and we fall into the deepest kiss. We've gone over together. *Together*. This is a word that was meaningless to me, and as I plunge my tongue inside her willing, open mouth again, I wonder how that could possibly be. Because now, it's everything.

Soon, I'm going to make it official.

SEVENTEEN

OLIVIA

When we wake in each other's arms, it's in the dawn of a new world. Nothing will ever be the same. I breathe in his manly, woodsy smell and close my eyes, feeling my lashes tickle against his tight, broad chest.

There is the urge to plant my stake in the ground and let the world know this man is mine. I'm giddy with the feel of him surging inside, still sticky with our lovemaking, and already eager to take him inside me again.

"Good morning, beautiful," he says, when his eyes blink open, little by little. I run my finger along his jaw, trace his full lower lip. He sucks my finger in, and it echoes with a throb between my legs. I slowly inch it out, then slip it back in, his licks and laps heavenly.

Suddenly, he turns me on my back and drapes his body over mine. His cock is throbbing, pressing into me. I part my legs, wrap them around him. We kiss like the night of sleep was too long to be apart. Between us, his crown and length tease and rub, the need to be connected that way everything. *On my knees, indeed.* I press my palms against his chest and toss him back.

"On my knees," I say, as I kneel on the floor and tug him into position.

His gaze is raw animal, his eyes dilated, passion and lust raw between us. His dick is massive, erect, and strong, and I wrap my hand around its base. He watches me. I'm so turned on by the rigid feel of him, the way he reacts to my sliding and tugging, the way I let my fingers caress his crown, gathering the wet droplet and spreading it over him.

Then I let my tongue in on the action. I swipe at his tip, make my tongue wide and run it back and forth over the top, then down one side and back up the other, caressing his balls as he calls out. Back at his crown, we lock eyes as I open wide and take in every inch of him. His hand presses my head as I glide him in and out, between my lips, applying a graze of my top teeth now and again as his breath catches.

I watch, mesmerized at the pleasure I'm bestowing upon him, the edge of ecstasy I'm dragging him along. He's so close, his thighs solid with the tension of built up sensation.

Suddenly, he slips his hands down to my waist, and raises me to standing. Aiden rises and tears open a condom packet. I watch as he unrolls it down his magnificent length. He presses me to him, his arms around my back, then in my hair, tugging.

He kisses me, licks and lashes so full of lust, I'm lost in them. He cups my ass and lifts me, spreading my legs, which I hug around him. I tilt my hips and he shifts, gliding into me. It's so deep and consuming, I'm afraid I'll be gone in seconds. Afraid I may never come back. And I couldn't give a fuck.

Within seconds, I'm throbbing and coming around him. "Come," I say. Because in that moment all that matters is feeling the sensation of him breaking apart under my touch, the same way he's done to me. "Come for me."

He stops, pulls his face back so we're eye to eye. "I—oh, I, you." He stops, thrusts. "You—" Then he judders. I feel the hot spurt as I groan and the condom fills between us. I'm blasted by aftershocks, my own body tightening and spasming around him.

We lay in that bed for hours, discovering every bit of each other. There's no mention of our hairbrained scheme. It's the bona fide Aiden and the bona fide Olivia, and I suspect he's also confounded by the real me, because I certainly am. She is better than any me I've known before, as if finally whole, complete.

We talk about everything. I hint at the "troubles" I've caused my parents. Though I don't quite get to the truth, I'm so close. I *want* to tell him. And that's new. Why would I *want* to make myself vulnerable to him that way? Because that's what love is. And I suspect, that's what *this* is.

EIGHTEEN

OLIVIA

The Q&A is held outside. Risers are set up so everyone has a seat. The whole company is up there. I'm in the front row, freshly showered, made up and hair styled. My body is raw and spent and heavy with being used as a vessel to chase the high of its new addiction: orgasm. Again and again.

Every innocent kiss and caress seemed to take us along that path. Desperate, we careened its increasingly sharp turns, its deeper drops, its exploration further and further still until every bit of each other had been claimed.

And now he leaves me with a kiss, our fingers entwined, slowly slipping from each other's as he backs away toward the long table on the stage. The separation smarts like a bruise. Is that because it is too good to last? Is it because having served each other's purposes and gotten caught up, we will now crash back into reality with a fatal thud?

The fear is new. And I'm smart enough to know it's the bedfellow of that vulnerability I was so desperate to bare for him.

I'm also smart enough to know that the way to deal with fear is to let it hang around, not to sweep it away, because such an effort will be fruitless. It shades everything, dims the world. But eventually you get used to it. The shade of dim becomes your usual shade and then, at least, you can get on with it.

Only now, getting on with it isn't enough. Not after Aiden. Living in the dim? Unthinkable. And the most dangerous bit? It's unlikely to ever suffice again. Which means lovers do whatever it takes to chase that feeling. And the way he's looking at me from his perch on the stage underlines our connection, proof it will only be that much worse when it's torn away.

The C.O.O., Charlie, speaks into the mic in front of him first. "Welcome, P.I.C. I trust you've been having an incredible conference. I certainly have. What about that Keith Dolan concert last night?"

There's a fair amount of cheering and clapping, but there's a shift in the air as all heads swivel my way.

Bless Charlie, he starts talking quickly. "And today is the famous Q&A session. A lot of CEOs wonder why we allow unscripted questions from each and every one of our employees. Anything and everything is on the table at these things. And I tell them it's because these unsaid issues are cancers to a company. They're the silent killers. There's nothing, and I mean *nothing*, you cannot ask Marc and Aiden Wheatley or myself today. So, who's gonna be first?"

The first question has to do with childcare and flexible working, and Aiden's answer is considered, fair, and generous. He's open to working from home, and he's not a fan of micro managing. "It's about hiring the right people you can trust," he says, "and then it's up to them to provide the results. When and how they go about getting there—as long as it's ethical and up to standard—is up to them."

There are questions about alternative 401K programs and about expanding into specific new markets. Marc defers most of them to Aiden, which I hadn't expected, and my lover fields them with respect, intelligence, and a natural curiosity, that makes me feel even closer to him. He genuinely promises to follow up, and I know I'm not the only one who is confident he will stand by his word.

The next person to be handed the microphone by the roving sound technician is Poppy. My posture stiffens as that huge ring of hers clunks the microphone, sending feedback through the air. I look to Aiden and his eyes are on me, protectively. His jaw is fixed tightly.

Poppy has a cat-who-ate-the-canary look as she shakes her hair out and prepares to speak. "Is it appropriate to hire someone you're in love with and pay them more than everyone else because of that fact?"

Aiden leans into the microphone and opens his mouth, then stops himself and looks at me. I know he wants to tell the truth, that I was hired before we ever met, that nothing had been happening before this weekend, that this was all for show. But I can't let him do that to himself. It's not fair. I'm sure that's why I shake my head once, sharply, squeeze my eyes in a silent plea, my intention unmistakable.

He nods in agreement.

NINETEEN

AIDEN

I t's so fucked up. I have to protect her, to tell the truth, say it wasn't real. But that would be an insult to what we have. Fuck it. I won't allow that truth to come out because people wouldn't understand. They'd think the worst and Olivia loses no matter what.

I don't give a fuck what they think about me in this moment. Olivia's too good for this and that's all I can think. "I would never act in the unethical way you're insinuating. In fact, I think we both know that the reason you're saying this right now has nothing to do with Olivia."

I leave it there. I will not sink to her level and slander her. Oh, I could. I could count the hundreds of emails and text messages she sent, begging me to see her again, show the world this crusade of hers is nothing more than the cold revenge of a woman scorned.

I could say, *Olivia certainly runs circles around you, Poppy, you awful, awful woman. She had the job before I ever knew her. I asked her to pretend to be my girlfriend to save face with my father. But that was all the bullshit of a terrified womanizer who realized he'd met the woman of his dreams, the woman he's going to make his wife.* But I won't. Aside from stooping to Poppy's level, it would certainly be the worst proposal in the history of the world.

Poppy tosses her head back and laughs. She actually believes she's winning here. I guess everyone has different ideas of success. I'm tracking Olivia, have no interest in anyone else here—not even Dad at the moment. She's a ball of disappointment, and it's worse than anger. Anger I could work with. But letting her down hits me like a ton of bricks.

"I believe you're acting unethically, not to mention unprofessionally, at this very moment, Poppy. We have not broken any rules. Furthermore, this is certainly not the place to wrongly accuse your peers, never mind your boss, of something so distasteful. I believe you'll find that's called slander—"

I'm in shock as I watch Olivia excuse her way past the others in the front row and double back to Poppy's place, halfway up the back. She takes the microphone from Poppy's hand. I know this woman I love—and make no mistake, I have never loved her more than I do in this moment—and she needs to speak, doesn't want me to stop her, which is just one of the million things that makes me love her.

Olivia scans the audience, Charlie and my father, then stops on me. She smiles hugely. I have to trust her. My body won't let me do anything else. "Aiden is nothing like you think. He's— well, he's got the kindest heart of anyone I've ever met. And he's, God, he's so manly, and just look at him. He's gorgeous. I tried to pretend, but I couldn't. I can't. This is all wrong. Because it's all right. I'm sorry." There are some chuckles.

But I know what it means for her to say those things—even if they don't quite make sense. I want to throw my arms around her. For now, I stand. In solidarity. I hope she feels me with her. Because I can't bear the idea that we'll ever be apart. Which in this moment feels inevitable.

"Mr. Wheatley, Marc—" She turns to my father.

He cocks his head, and what a smile he flashes her. She wouldn't realize how she's cut through to him with her honesty, because she was just being herself. If any other person on the planet had been responsible for turning this conference into such a *shemozzle*, he'd have their head . . . no matter how beautiful it might be.

"I understand Aiden has had his fair share of, of, *dalliances*." More giggles. A couple of hoots. "But he's so much more than that. You wouldn't believe what he's gone through to impress you." She doesn't even mention the stretched truth I gave her about my father disinheriting my shares of the company if I didn't have a stable relationship by this conference. God love her. Makes me feel even worse for making that up.

Back then, before I fell for Olivia, the only reason I cared to find someone serious had been for Dad's respect and his respect alone. Did she instinctively get that about me? If so, it's the biggest compliment I've ever had. And it's certainly part of the reason that nothing matters now—not even my father's view—but her. I'm not going to let her go.

She looks back to the sea of people. "I'm sorry for the trouble I caused," she says. "I hope you can forgive me."

"I don't think so," Poppy says. *Bitch*. I've never hit a girl, but bloody hell, do I feel like breaking that streak.

Something snaps in me, and I can't leave her to stand there alone for another second. I make my way to Olivia and take the microphone from her hand, hand it to the tech. Then I take her face in my hands and kiss her for all the company to see.

My father is going to kill me, but in that moment, I don't give a shit. Just want Olivia to know how incredible she is, how incredible she makes me feel, and that I don't plan on giving it up easily, whatever she may have in mind, with that terrifyingly hopeless look on her face.

This is not the passionate kiss I had in mind. She's frozen, trying not to respond to my kiss. Despite this, we get a standing ovation, but this only seems to make Olivia more determined than ever to flee. She tries to escape from my grip, but I reach for her hand and escort her out of the room. We are in this together. I want my arm firmly around her waist to say it. Only that hand has never said such a thing to a woman before, and I can't be sure I'm getting it right. Her body language certainly hints that I'm not.

Her face is all kinds of red. I can't help but love her more for walking out in the middle of all that. However, I fear she's walking out on more than the company, and I'm not ready for that. The idea that she'd walk out on me when I've opened up to her, done everything I could to protect her and show her how I feel is brewing into a rage inside me.

"Well, that went pretty well, I think," I say to break the tension and slow the anger building in my chest. And just think, I had planned to propose to her at that Q&A. Just goes to show that life never ceases to shock the hell out of you.

TWENTY

OLIVIA

I am bubbling with anger. That was humiliating and even worse, made me feel so angry on Aiden's behalf. Even though I had stopped him from being out with it, when I, myself, started to spill it with that painfully public speech, I found I couldn't bring myself to explain what was fake. Was it ever really fake?

I take one look at him, having left that group of people that are his company, his father, his life, with me, to defend my honor, and I know it's as real as ever. I want him. And I suspect he wants me. But I've been wrong before. And I've risked that for him. Sure, I wanted to protect him, but I was also terrified: I couldn't risk the possibility of him stating, straight-faced in front of all those people that we were putting on a show. And I knew he was going to.

"I appreciate what you did in there. I really do," I hear myself say. "But that can't happen again. It's never going to be anything but tawdry and tainted now." Oh, I recognize those words of mine. They are the kind that lay that protective layer between me and the rest of the world, the kind sickly kids learn to heft around to get by without feeling like they miss out on everything.

And later, when it turns out all that fighting has helped them to live through it all, well, then they've got no idea what they really feel, how to read what other people feel, because they've missed too much.

There are three people on this planet I trust: Mom, Dad, and my best friend Jo. But even with them, I have to act. It's a small price to pay for all the sacrifices they've made for me. I do it for them, I'd always thought. But in this moment, I'm not sure. It feels a hell of a lot like fear speaking.

"Oh, come on, Olivia. This is not you talking. This is all those people who think you get by because you're pretty. This is you watching out for me. But I don't want you to do that, which is why I wanted to be out with it. If I had to choose between everything else in my life and you, I'd choose you. I've only known you for a few days and I'm already certain of that."

"Do you hear yourself, Aiden? This is romantic nonsense." *He's so dead-on, it's not even funny. If he had all the information —the truth about my former health problems—he'd be one hundred percent correct. But from what he had to work with, the man's got me pretty well pegged.*

And yet, I keep toeing the line to ending it all. "You can't just walk away from your whole world in real life. And you shouldn't have to. Come on. We both know this is too good to last. It's, well, it's indescribable. It's not made for this world. How can something like this ever survive in the kind of world where Poppy walks the earth?"

"Hey," he says, his hands at my face, gentle, loving in the most honest way. "I should have told you about Poppy. I deeply regret giving into her advances. The old Aiden sometimes got off on showing people he was exactly as despicable as they liked to paint him. But you've made me better than that."

"Oh please, Aiden. In three days? Nobody changes like that."

"Love does crazy things to people."

"I think you've got that wrong. When things get crazy, people think they're in love."

I can see the hurt in his eye. Immediately, I want to take it back. But I'm too far gone. And already I can feel my defenses kicking in, saying: *this is for the best. The world is not a happy place. Much better off living that as your truth.*

I make myself walk away from him. My chest freezes with the realization that he lets me go. Getting what you want isn't ever what it's cracked up to be.

He calls after me. "I can't win with you, Olivia." His voice is cold, unfeeling, like he's given up. And though this is what my words had been convincing him to do, hearing him do so is unbearable.

I don't turn around.

"Are you going to run scared every time things get hard?"

My heart is pounding, blood rushing in my ears. I don't speak. It appears he's not the only one who's shut down. Instead I start walking again.

"You know what that makes you, Olivia?"

Now, at the elevator doors, I turn back to hear the awful truth I can sense he's about to hurl at me.

"It makes you a coward."

The doors open and I step inside, my chest heaving. He stares me down with an icy look that sends shivers up my spine.

TWENTY-ONE
AIDEN

When our expectations don't match the outcome of a situation, our brain sounds an alarm in the little area called the amygdala. The result is anger.

I know this from when I was a schoolboy. I couldn't do anything about my parents fighting, couldn't even protect my brother from hearing it, so I got really good at getting angry. So good that after getting in trouble in school too many times, the headmaster made me talk to a counselor.

I eventually learned to do something to take my mind off the anger. But what I learned to do was women. And that is absolutely no good to me at the moment.

"Fuck this!" I yell for the final time. I've paced my suite so many times, I'm surprised I haven't worn away the carpet. But I can't calm down. Caring too much to run off and screw my emotions to bits is new, and I don't know what to do with myself.

There's a knock at the door.

"Go away!" I yell.

"Aiden, it's Dad. Let me in."

He's the last person I should be in the same room with right now. I'll start blaming him for all my shortcomings and then I'll be an even bigger dick than I am.

I growl, but I go to the door all the same. This is not an Aiden I recognize—one who admits to himself he needs help and literally opens the door to it.

"You look like shit," he says. It's not an insult. It's the way we talk to each other.

"Thanks," I say.

"That was some show. That woman of yours has got guts, son. I don't know where you found her, but she's one in a million."

I look at him and feel a chill creep up my back. He's right. And I called her a coward. Fuck, I'm a dick. It was the pot calling the kettle black. Because the reality was, I wanted to say the truth about us in that Q&A, but when Olivia shook her head, I was *relieved*. I didn't want to make either of us look like fools. But it would have been the right thing to do *for our relationship*. She was protecting me, that's why she shook her head. And I knew it. A better man would have been out with it. A man who wasn't scared to death at himself using the word *relationship*.

"I said some unkind things to her after all that Q&A debacle."

"We all say unkind things, Aiden. The key is to be man enough to make it right afterward, to treat her well always, so that when you have a bad moment like that, she knows you didn't mean it."

He looks meaningfully at me. There's subtext there and he wants me to understand that.

I dip my chin. It meant a lot for him to say that. I think of what I've learned from Olivia, how deeply her honesty brought us together. He's opened the pathway and it's up to me to tell him the truth. It's the only thing that has the power to bring us closer, to mend old wounds.

I take a huge, preparatory breath, exhale it. "Dad, I knew there was something between Olivia and me from the moment I saw her."

"You'd have to be an idiot not to."

I smile. This lightness between us is new. And it feels good. Makes it easier to say what I have to say.

"But the night I met her, I was in a different headspace than I am now. I wanted to show you that I was not like you. I wanted to show you that I could be a better man than you."

My eyes trace his reaction. It hurts to hear these things, I'm sure.

"And that was my motivation behind saying I'd have a serious relationship by this conference."

He nods slowly, his eyes laser-focused on me.

"And before Olivia was in the picture, I was prepared to put on a show with a woman I didn't care one iota for, just to prove that to you. Which makes me everything I was angry at you for."

Now it's his turn to take huge breaths. There's so much pain in the rise and fall of his chest, it shocks me.

"Oh Aiden. I'm so glad you told me that. I know the pain I've caused you. And I know it has been the driving force behind many of your worst behaviors and traits. You've always been so angry."

"Unlike Finn, who can somehow magically forgive and forget."

"It's not magic, Aiden."

I cock my head. "No?"

"No. Let me tell you something. One night your mother and I were having a knock-down, drag-out fight. It was my fault, of course. I was a serial cheater. Of course, she was angry. But I was so truly selfish. I always found a reason to defend myself.

"Hours after, we both threw in the towel, because there was never going to be a solution, I found you and Finn asleep under a pillow and blanket fort you'd erected in the closet overnight because you couldn't stand us fighting. You were sharing a pair of headphones and you had your arms wrapped around him so tightly.

"*I* made you protective of him, angry on his behalf. And you protecting him that way and providing security is precisely why he's been able to forgive and find genuine happiness. Because of you."

There's a ring of truth to that, which sends shivers down my back. A life-changing kind of truth.

"Thank you, Dad."

"Now listen. Don't be angry with Olivia. She was humiliated and it must have played with insecurities that have nothing to do with you—a pretty girl like her, she's bound to have had lots of haters in her life. Be the hero. This situation is made for it."

"Dad, if you know all this, understand people like you do, then why don't you go out there and get some of this love for yourself?"

"Me? That knowledge has been hard-won. I've hurt the people I love too much in this life to ever risk it again. I will never forget that night, seeing your arms wrapped around your brother. I'd done that to you. Your mother and I divorced soon after."

I reach my hand out and place it firmly on his shoulder. "Those words really mean a lot."

He's holding back how chuffed he is because that's the way Marc Wheatley operates. And I've just shot him with a sample of Olivia honesty that is brand new to us. But I got my old blue eyes from him, and I know how to read their nuances. It's the happiest I've seen him in my life.

"I love you, Dad. And I probably do a bit too much to show you I'm a good man." I don't say, *not like you*, because, suddenly I don't feel that way anymore. And letting go of that anger feels like a ten-ton weight has been lifted.

"Now, go get that woman. You and I both know she's too good for you." It's good to see he can still be his snarky self after all that unloading between us, so I smile. "If you let her alone too long to work that out, you'll really be in trouble. Jack took her to the car rental agency by the airport."

TWENTY-TWO

OLIVIA

In an hour, I'm alone (blessedly, I keep failing to convince myself) at a car rental office huddled over my wheely luggage to hide the red hue that won't leave my face. I'm going to have to tell my parents the truth. It will break their hearts. That's just how it has to be. At least concentrating on that distracts me from the way Aiden looked when I walked away in that hallway, from the way I kept looking at the door of the suite for him to come in and talk me out of this.

I want to go home early from the conference, rent a car, and get on the open road with my thoughts. The rental agency doesn't have anything but a giant van unless I wait "a little while." So, on the pleather bench, I wait. It's nothing like the first class travel I enjoyed on the way here. And with no privacy, it makes it difficult to wallow in my misery the way I really want to.

I look at the facts: What we shared in bed was real. What he did for me with Keith Dolan was real. And what he said to the company was real. Then he told me he loved me. And how did I thank him? I told him he did not.

Three hours later, my anger is white hot. Had I expected he'd come after me?

So, why did it piss me off so badly that he was going to tell everyone our narrative was fake? And why was I pretending that didn't bother me, that I was only against a confession to save his reputation?

Because I'd drunk the Kool-Aid. I'd tried to walk the tightrope between fake and real, but it turned out I couldn't hack it in the face of Mr. Gorgeous Generous Billionaire. It was much safer when he was just Wet Shirt (as if he was ever *just* anything).

Toss my favorite musician at me, bring me to orgasm seven times, call me beautiful, and I fall into the trap of all good women, everywhere—believing in the illusion of love. And now I'd made a fool of myself in front of the entire company too. Talk about going down in flames. In some ways, this is worse than the Corey screw-up. And the hateful words I said to him, the hateful words he said to me. Could they ever be taken back?

Where had I expected we'd end up with this ludicrous charade? Despite what I'm feeling, it *was* fake—a dumb, deceitful plan to . . . To not so much save my parents from pain as to save myself from being seen as the giant disappointment I identify as.

I've fallen for him. A gorgeous billionaire with a heart of gold and a sparkling wit, what had I expected? That this would finally be exactly what it felt like from the second he'd touched my cheek with that serviette—my happily ever after?

My mother has a radar for my emotions and on cue, my mobile rings the silly ringtone she chose, so I'd always know it was her—Buzz Lightyear from Toy Story crooning *To Infinity and Beyond!*

I smile despite myself. She's got the Facetime video option

selected, so as I accept her call, I brace myself and plaster on a grin.

"Hello!" she says. She's cut her hair and it looks godawful. The bangs (*fringe* as they would say here) are way too short and she looks like a frightened child. This tiny thing finally makes me think I may cry. Perhaps the tears would shake free some of the anger.

"Mom! You cut your hair. It's good."

She inclines her head. "Don't lie. You know I hate when you lie."

Oh, that is not sitting well at the moment.

"It's terrible. I don't know how long it's going to take to grow out."

She lifts a lock and squints her eyes. "What's wrong with you?"

"Nothing!" My voice is too high. It's the pressure of a woman who knows you and loves you boundlessly. Is it any wonder I want to please her, want to be anything other than a drain on her life? Just look at her with those ridiculous bangs!

"Do *not* lie to me. Is it Corey? Did he do something?"

It is truly terrifying the way she can do this. "Of course not! Corey is—well, he's Corey, as Corey as always."

She doesn't seem to know how to take this.

"Olivia?" How does she do that with just my name? Wrap it in all her care and worry? I want to confess everything. God, I want a hug from her. She gives the best hugs; they make me feel like I'm seven years old again.

She used to sleep in my hospital bed with me. She'd use my belly as her pillow and I'd pretend it hurt, but when she'd move, I'd yank her back. She even managed to make it fun. She'd bring DVDs and we'd erect a blanket fort and gorge on marshmallows and chocolate.

But I can't give into a childish need like that. I remember

how thin Mom became back then, how she had smiled her ass off, but it would never quite make it to her eyes. Whenever I caught her unawares, she'd look so worried, exhausted. She gave up her career, everything for me. I will not burden this lovely woman with the terrible bangs anymore. I'm happy enough. And if I'm not, I'll get there before she sees for herself.

"It's fine, Mom. Corey's excited for your trip. We were just talking about taking you to our local pub because they make the best fish and chips."

I breathe in, realizing I haven't for some moments, when I smell something stupidly sexy linger on the inhale. I breathe it in like an addict. I know before I look up from my phone that it's Aiden. What the actual fuck? I want to look angry, but it comes out as a smile. He came to rescue me. Like a knight in shining armor.

And what is so fucking wrong with me liking that? If we're being honest here, *loving that*. And not least of all because he was able to bypass my words to know what I really wanted. It's such a relief to have someone who really knows me and who— whether by their sheer will rather than my own—I can actually lean on. I feel a world of tension leave my body.

"Ah! Corey's just arrived, hasn't he? There's no mistaking that smile on your face."

Aiden lets one side of his mouth raise in a cocky grin.

"Yup! I have to go, Mom."

"Okay! I love you! Can't wait to see you! Hopefully my hair grows out by then. Otherwise I'm wearing one of your old wigs!"

Oh, there's so much in that exchange I wish he hadn't heard. It's like the second you even *think* of leaning on someone, all your dirty laundry is shoved out the window onto their head. That quickly, I feel the tightness creep back into my shoulders.

I hang up, taking my time returning the phone to my pocket, to avoid Aiden's inquisitive gaze.

"How did you know I was here?" I ask, standing. I feel too vulnerable and sitting in the shadow of Mr. Tall, Dark and Handsome is just too much.

"I had Jack take me. Why would I want to be there if you aren't around?"

I study him and there is no irony there. "You don't have to pretend now, Aiden. Nobody's here that cares." I hear the anger in my voice. He said he loved me. What is this drivel I'm spewing? Don't I know it's only because the real feelings have obliterated the fake ones? We're stepping around the dirty laundry and he's not going anywhere.

"Hey, I owe you an enormous apology. You are anything but a coward. You are the bravest, most wonderful woman I've ever met. And if you let me, I will never do anything that makes you say a negative word about me again. I don't even want you to apologize for what you said. I know you didn't mean it. You know how I feel about you. It's scary. I get it. I'm scared too. But it's real and you know it. And neither of us are going to even *think* the word fake again."

He is here, saying everything I want to hear. How can I do anything but jump into his arms, let his love wash over me? The feel of his fingers smoothing my hair finally brings the tears.

When I step back, he sweeps a palm over my cheek. "I know that was uncomfortable for you today," he says.

"Uncomfortable? Is a colonoscopy uncomfortable? That was freaking awful. Never been so humiliated in my life! And that includes when Corey was mounting that woman in my bed."

"It was wrong, what Poppy said."

The sound of her name on his lips makes me tingle with anger. He has a past, sure. But that doesn't mean I have to like it.

"And I can't even begin to tell you how sorry I am that I ever had anything to do with that woman. I wanted to tell the truth about us. But you stopped me. I knew you had your reasons, and I had my reasons too. But I should have been out with it. That was fear holding both of us back. But I don't want to be afraid anymore. You make me face these things holding me back."

"Me?"

"Just by being you, you make me a better me."

"It would be worse if you told the truth. We'd be a complete laughingstock! And your father will disinherit your shares of the company."

He hesitates, parts those luscious lips, but takes his time before speaking. "You care about me, don't you?"

"No!"

"No?"

"No!"

He pulls me close and looks me in the eyes so deeply all the wind is knocked out of me.

"Forgive me?" he asks.

I nod, my eyes glassy. "Forgive me?" I say, my chin quivering.

"Always. Nothing's worth it without you. I meant what I said." He doesn't say the L word, but we both know what he means.

"No more faking," he says.

He kisses me deeply, and I melt into a puddle. *Yes,* my tongue is saying, dancing with his, thrusting as deep inside of him as I can. And yet, I'm keeping something from him.

"Mmmm-hmmm," he says when our mouths part, slowly, sensually, a lower lip between his teeth for a long moment before we let go.

"You know, it's emasculating not to let a man come to your rescue."

"Well, maybe you need a little emasculating. You know there's such a thing as too masculine." Even as I say it, I don't believe it myself. Aiden is all man and it's irresistible.

He just nods. "It'll be a great story."

"What do you mean?"

"The way we started out."

I want to tell him to stop, but I love the way it sounds. He reaches for my hand and leads me to the check-in desk. "Miss Barker won't be needing that car anymore."

"Yes, Mr. Wheatley."

Aiden puts my bag in his trunk, rejecting the chauffeur's offer to do so. "Now, are we going to take that vineyard tour we talked about, or not?"

TWENTY-THREE

AIDEN

That ring is burning a hole in my pocket. It figures that the first time in my life I want to propose, I actually can't do it. There's never been a worse setup for a proposal in the history of marriage.

The funny thing is I am *never* off my game. And I mean never. But at this moment, riding through the streaky orange and purple Hunter Valley sky, the grape scent wafting through the open windows, her hand in mine, I don't know which end is up.

We were faking; then we were furious at the idea we were faking. Now we're not faking. I get it, but I want to put it out there, make it real. The idea of that just makes me love her even more.

We pull up the drive to a vineyard whose sign features a galloping horse, alongside the words "Cockfighter's Ghost." I'm aware of the off-color jokes the name conjures, but when she hears the story about the eponymous horse who lost its life in this area and haunts it still, she'll get it. And if there are a few cock jokes along the way, I can live with that.

God bless her, I see her eyes dance and a smile float over her lips, but she quickly restrains it.

I laugh.

"What?"

"Nothing," I say, squeezing her fingers.

The chauffeur pulls up past the statue of the horse to the cellar door building, an unassuming steel structure with a heavenly view of the hills and vines.

He knows I want to open the car doors myself and gives me the nod in the rearview. I exit first and walk around to open Olivia's door. She steps out, her slim dark pants and sheer blouse showing off her extraordinary curves.

Inside, there are cheery yellow accents, a chalkboard, and all sorts of homely decorations, and I can tell right away that she loves the place. I'm so glad to be the one to show it to her. *Maybe you can fix this after all.*

They've been expecting us, so we get a warm welcome from one of the winemakers, a bloke in the kind of getup you'd expect —an old Akubra hat, worn-in grape-stained jeans, and a faded tee shirt that shows off all the years his arms spent exposed in the Australian sun.

"Jim Jones," he says, tapping his hat by way of hello.

He leads us to a tall table with a couple of stools and some nibbles and a ton of wine glasses in every shape. Olivia's shoulders bounce in excitement. Her eyes are aglow. I cannot wait to see her moan over the Shiraz. Operation Proposal is off to a cracking start.

Jim pours the first glass, talking about vanilla and fig, jammy notes—all that wanker stuff I happen to think is irrelevant unless you're trying to sell the bloody thing, which he is. All I know is we clink our oversize glasses, swirl according to Jimbo's direction, and the smell is incredible as the alcohol clings to the sides of the glass.

We're in for a treat. And by *we*, I mean me and Jimbo, because we get to watch this glorious gem enjoy this quaff for the first time (yeah, I know all the wanker language, can even pull it out if it makes for a good turn of phrase, or more importantly, makes Olivia smile.).

She's done this before. I can tell because she sticks her nose in and sniffs, pulls the glass away and then does it again, enjoying the distinct notes in a hint of the way she enjoyed my grinding into her in ecstasy.

I get a flash of what those hips look like under those pants. My cock stiffens. She gently lifts her glass and lets the ruby liquid glide past her lips. Her eyes close and I throb with need. I look at Jim with the politest fuck-off look I can muster. He can't help it after all. He's only human.

"Holy hell, that is good."

"I think I just found my new spokeswoman," Jimbo says, and what must pass for his smile slightly raises one corner of his lips.

"Oh no, you don't," I say. "She's *my* spokeswoman. Skyrocketing *my* stock."

Olivia cocks her head. "That's very kind of you to say."

"I'm not being *kind*, Olivia. I'm telling the truth."

Jimbo discreetly goes to tend to something behind the bar. Rich people put out that kind of signal and it's instantly obeyed. I know I take it for granted, but that's the way it's been all my life.

I do appreciate the power my family yields, but that's also what's created the kind of immense pressure that brought me to fake-date Olivia, when what I should have done was *real* date her.

But that freaked her out at the hotel, obviously, which is why she wouldn't let me play her knight in shining armor and get the truth out in front of the entire company. That and the fact that she clearly felt as comfortable in that situation as she would with a medical instrument up her rectum.

I'm not sure another woman could get away with saying the word *colonoscopy* and still have me wanting to bend her over the bar and slide in from behind. But here we are. My achingly hard cock is proof of that.

She takes another thoughtful sip, letting her lips smack as she swallows. This is not good for my blood flow.

She looks like she wants to say something but doesn't.

I lean in. "We said we're going to be honest, right? What were you going to say?"

Her chest heaves. She studies my face but still doesn't speak.

"Come on, Olivia."

"I just, well, I wondered what really happened with Poppy."

I've been expecting this.

Her shoulders droop. "You slept with her." Her eyes blink rapidly.

"You're jealous."

"What? Of course, I'm not jealous! You're a lothario. You admitted it yourself. That's why you asked me to pretend to be your girlfriend. Sure, you may have done some incredibly thoughtful things that have blurred the reality, but Poppy helped to put it all in stark relief. She's done me a favor, really. Made it all *real*."

"Then why is your eye twitching?" I flash my best panty-dropping smile.

It doesn't work. Which, I can guess means she really is jealous, which means she cares, but also doesn't jive with her body language.

"It is not *twitching*! I—I just got something stuck in it."

"Yeah, me."

She removes her palm from her eye and shoots me a look

that could melt icebergs. Her mouth opens, but nothing comes out. Her lips close with a pop.

"Look, I could have killed Poppy for treating you with such disrespect. She will most certainly be reprimanded and put on a warning. That is bullying behavior. According to work policy, we've done nothing wrong, and I stand behind that.

"Besides, I could find someone to do her job in a minute. You are paid what you are worth. In fact, now I've met you, you probably should be paid double. But that might get me into trouble."

"Why?" she asks.

"*Why?* Because *look* at you. All I want to do is tear your clothes off. You have to understand people would be dubious."

She leans back on her stool with a sigh. "I do. Been dealing with it my whole life. Even at college, the girls hated me. They were your typical geeky or mod girls, the kind you would expect to be programming, and they took one look at me and decided I was stupid. Didn't have one girlfriend the whole four years."

"Bet you had lots of boyfriends, though. Didn't you?"

Oh, it feels good to be the cause of that glittering smile.

I feel for the ring box in the pocket of my jeans. I wave Jimbo back over. It's time for him to reemerge and pretend he didn't hear any of that. Olivia is squirming and I can tell she isn't comfortable with the idea of what he'd witnessed. I put my hand on hers.

"Trust me?" I ask.

TWENTY-FOUR

OLIVIA

O h, he's up to something. I don't know what it is, but the crinkles around his eyes have become crinklier. And the blue has taken on a murkiness that I could try to decode all day. He's saying important stuff, but not in a concrete way. So, I *think* I know what he means, but I can't be one hundred percent sure.

I'm seeing a theme in our relationship and it is not one that sits easy with me. Data Girl with data that cannot be trusted. And yet, there's a yearning inside me that defies all logic. I have a feeling logic would be the absolute death of this burning passion that has consumed me since that first kiss at the hotel. It's terrifying, but in a delicious way that I know can only mean trouble. Hence the worry about the increased eye crinkles.

"We're meant to be going to the next vineyard, but I'm having such a good time here, I thought we might stay a bit longer. We can order some food from the restaurant if you like?"

I nod. There is a special, simply joyful atmosphere here that seems to ease the tension and zero in on the positives of our connection.

Jim brings over a couple menus and offers his recommendations, which we take. We're alone as he shuffles over to the restaurant to put in the order.

"Hey, can I ask you something personal?" Aiden says.

I try to gulp a huge breath. This is about what he overheard during my phone call with Mom. What are the chances of him walking in at the exact moment she was saying that? "What was your mum was saying about wigs?"

I close my eyes. I didn't want him to know about this. I don't want anyone to know about this. I don't want to know about this. It's the reason my parents have been to hell and back, and it's the reason I feel guilty about this transcontinental move falling to shit. And yet, I have been aching to unburden myself on him, an ache I have done everything possible to ignore.

Lungs, asthma, infections, kidney. You name it and it's a common problem for premature babies who make it past the first danger zone. As we get older, depression is a major risk, and when I felt the first pangs of that, so early in my teen years, what I did was get all the facts.

If I didn't have the will to live through this, I never would, and what would that do to my parents? I understood that loud and clear, and knew I wouldn't put them through that. The research and fact compiling I did then was how I wound up getting into data science.

I became obsessed with getting a clear picture of all the risks. And once I'd mapped them out—all over my bedroom walls to my mother's dismay—I felt like I had a clearer picture of the elements I *could* control, even understanding those I *couldn't* control eased my anxiety.

I explain all that to Aiden. "It started out as something I did for my parents. They were always so worried. Mom had to quit her job because she was always having to take time off for my unexpected hospital stays, illnesses that would never quite leave me.

"I've taken exceptional care of myself my whole life because I understood how this could give me the edge in survival. And I've been lucky too. At points in my life, my lungs have failed me, my kidneys, you name it. And yes, I've lost my hair from medications I had to take. But we managed to get through it. I haven't had a health issue in over four years."

"But your parents weren't convinced when you wanted to follow Mr. Dickwad all the way to Australia."

"Bingo. Get the guy another Shiraz." I pour him a generous glass. We've each had about three by now, and I realize I'm probably more loose-lipped than I would be otherwise. It also feels incredible to get this off my chest—to *him*.

"And you don't want to break their hearts again by telling them the truth about how it all went down when you got here."

I tap the side of my glass, realizing I'm more than a little bit tipsy. "Ding ding ding!" I say.

"And that's where I come in, showing them I'm the man who's so much better than Corey that they'll be so happy they won't know what to do with themselves."

"*Pretending* you're that man."

He lifts his arm and looks at his watch, incredulity in his face. "You made it two hours," he says, leaning in. "Didn't we just say no more pretending?"

I'm tongue tied. "I'm sorry." I try my best puppy dog eyes.

It works, he laughs, shaking his head. "You need to work on that look. I can see you don't have much practice with that sort of thing, but hey, sometimes, it's an excellent tool." He reaches out and rubs at my palm reassuringly.

"Thank you," I say.

"What for?" he says.

"Your patience."

"My pleasure, beautiful." He takes my face in his hands over the small barrel table and kisses me. His lips are lush and as soft as I remember, and they take control in a way that makes me instantly damp.

There's his tongue, claiming what's his, and, boy, do I want it to be—his and no one else's. My spine tingles, I lean in, run my hands through his hair. *It's not pretend*, I assure myself.

When he slowly slips his tongue from my mouth, still holding me near, his gaze echoes my reassurance, just in case I had trouble believing it, trusting myself to go with it. My heart thumps. I'm going to face any fears and make this work. He deserves nothing less.

And then his deep voice says something purely Aiden. "If you get off on pretending, I've got some other ideas we could play out."

I swat at him, but his words have a hint of truth in them, the way we weaved in and out of the honesty of our feelings, added a whole other level of unexpected eroticism. And while our bodies peaked in honesty, our hearts and words rode that high. It's how we go to this intense point so quickly.

"Here's something that's no joke, though." His face looks so sad, I almost want to take back the things I've just confessed. "I am so glad you shared all that with me. It is my honor to be your confidante, one of the great honors of my life. Give me all your hurt, Olivia, and I will turn it into something bright and beautiful, something to reflect what you give to me."

I'm speechless. It's the most caring, gorgeous thing a person has ever said to me—maybe to anyone.

Jim comes back with three artfully plated tapas-sized dishes and a couple of linen napkins folded into perfect squares. There's a salmon tartare, a teepee of tempura vegetables with a divine looking dipping sauce and a couple of duck pancakes.

The international take on food in Australia is a balance of sophisticated and simple, as if all the cultures of the world were meant to meld in just this way. The beautiful, fresh Pacific seafood elevates things to a whole new level. But seeing them through the lens of the words Aiden has just spoken, they look like priceless treasures. It makes me realize I need to say something.

"You are a surprising, wonderful man, Aiden Wheatley. And you make me incredibly happy."

The look he gives me as his fingers graze my cheek says it all. It powers our kiss with a passion unlike anything I've experienced before. When we part, we tuck in and I guzzle the water Jimbo has just poured from the carafe into my glass. I need to slow down on the alcohol and try to make sense of what's just been shared between us.

I start in on the salmon first. It's divine, and the cream they've dolloped alongside is sublime. Before I know it, I've nearly finished it all.

"Aren't you going to have any?" I say.

"It's much more fun watching you enjoy it."

"Suit yourself," I say, smoothing some cream on the last sliver of salmon and lifting it to my mouth. I'm feeling sheepish, like I've said too much. I never talk about my medical issues. Corey never had a clue, and probably that was a bit unfair. I just could never bring myself to let him see my weakness. I certainly didn't expect talking about them to bring us this close.

Yet, I'm light, and bright, and feeling closer to Aiden than I've ever felt to another man. I'm beginning to see that the vulnerability I've been so afraid of is intricately embroidered into this beautiful, weave of our connection. It's the balance that's the ultimate difference between love and hate. Are we to be the lucky ones who get it right?

TWENTY-FIVE

AIDEN

"That's quite a burden you've been carrying around," I say to Olivia after she finishes the last of the salmon. "You think your parents would be happy to know you've been living your life in a way to ensure that it's least painful for them? I mean, my father would, but it doesn't sound like they're from the same species."

She lets out a sigh that could inflate a pool. "Aiden, you just don't understand what it's like knowing you're putting your parents through hell every single day, that their entire lives have been hijacked by you and all your health needs. And finally, when I've gotten to the point where I can give them some breathing room, have taken the burden from their shoulders, I'll have to say, 'Hey! Just kidding! I *can't* take care of myself. Look at how badly I fucked everything up.'"

She sniffs loudly and I can tell she's fighting like anything to hold back tears. I admire that. She's not looking for a shoulder to cry on, though I would give my life to be that shoulder any time she needed it.

I lean in close over the nearly empty plates, take her hand in a way that is anything but fake. "Olivia—" she meets my gaze, "did you come to Australia so that your parents could have a break? Am I right in saying you didn't even love Corey, just thought this was the perfect way to free them from the burden of you?"

"Though I've never even admitted this to myself, yes, Aiden, that is absolutely why I came here. And you know what? It was easy to be angry at Corey for it not working out. But the truth is it wouldn't have worked out anyway, unless I stayed with someone I wasn't in love with."

She can see the surprise on my face, I'm sure. Because she waves her hands and says, "See? Data Girl is an inconsistent bag of ironies! Makes no sense at all outside of a spreadsheet! There you have it! The truth! You can, and probably should, just go right back to pretending. Now you have a real reason to want nothing to do with me."

I stand and come around to her side of the table, gently pull her off the stool so she's standing, then I get down on one knee. "Complete opposite actually. Just makes me want you more. I was going to do this today during the Q&A, but that just didn't seem like the right time with the whole Poppy debacle."

She smiles and shoots me a look that says, *ya think?*

"But now, seeing this real you, I think we should take this whole fake relationship to the next level. Will you be my fiancée?"

Her eyes bulge. She doesn't know what to make of this, especially since I just told her it wasn't a fake relationship and now I'm using that terminology—the one she seems able to deal with before she can trust herself to know it's real—and that's exactly my plan.

She studies me like a map. "You mean *fake* fiancée?"

I cock my head in a way that she can interpret as yes if that's what she needs to do.

"But that's crazy! How are you ever going to get out of this without a whole world of nasty if you take it that far? Shouldn't we just enjoy this new level of honesty we've created before we throw a cyclone of mind-bending fiction or reality into it?"

"In for a penny, in for a pound, isn't that what they say?"

"Is that like 'you've fucked it up this badly already, might as well burn the whole thing down?'"

I laugh. And then I can't help it. I pull her in for a kiss, my arms wrapped tightly around her. I'm so sure I *get* her. And who knew such a thing could feel like all the riches in the world? If this ridiculous paradigm helps her ease into the reality of our happiness, I'm honored to be the man to create it for her.

"I don't want you to answer now. Spend the day and night with me. Then let's talk about it in the morning. But please put this ring on because I do not want to lose it."

I slip it onto her finger, knowing I've struck the right tone. She looks lighter already. And I'm so glad. I know how much it cost her to share her greatest fears with me. "And it looks so much better on you than it does in the box. Besides, you'll be indulging me. I like people to see you're mine. Nobody can miss it with the size of this thing."

She looks at the ring, then at me. Then back at the ring and to me again. She doesn't know whether to bolt or take me into the men's room. She's abso-fucking-lutely gorgeous. She'll be wearing that ring for all the right reasons. I just need her to trust me. And to give her the time to feel comfortable about what we both knew from that first time our shoulders brushed at the bar.

Because right now, this woman who had never been ready to trust anyone has put more trust in me than she's put in any man before. And I want to be the man that fixes all that for her for good.

TWENTY-SIX
OLIVIA

The world's largest rock has wound up on my finger. And look as I might from it to the man who slipped it on there, it refuses to make any sense. I've just had the only meltdown in front of a man—perhaps another living human that isn't in a nurse's uniform—that I've ever had in my life. And the answer is that he puts a ring on it. If I needed another reason to run, this is certainly it. Aiden's judgment is one hundred percent fucked—and I have the data on that. And yet, here I am.

"I suppose it doesn't matter whether I want to be your fiancée?" I'm saying it, but my brain has also just caught up, and his hand is rubbing so sweetly on my shoulder, like he wants to be the person to share this burden we've just been discussing, and any other problem I ever have with me. Yes, a hand saying all that.

My lady parts weigh in and they go completely molten. So much so that when his soft lips touch mine, I feel crazy, like I could hide behind the bar Jim just vacated and rip Aiden's clothes off.

Then he confuses it even more because he stands me up, continues to press his tongue against mine in a kiss that seems to undermine the word *fake* at every turn, that is so sure of what it wants and what I want, and is terrifyingly correct. Aiden takes things to nuclear with an embrace that is so strong and comforting and, well, *loving*—as ridiculous as that is—that the fucking tears pour. I can't help them.

As soon as he realizes, he pulls back, touches his cheek to mine, and sweetly, perfectly, traces his finger to catch the tears. I watch him doing this and it's so soothing and calming, cracking opening and releasing this pressure, accepting this comfort from him, that I am literally in shock. *You need this man.* Fuck off, I do not. And yet...

"Listen, beautiful, if you want to take the ring off for your parents' visit, you can do that. Just test it out for my end of the bargain. After today's fiasco, if you aren't going to let me tell the truth, we need to make this official."

"Doesn't something about this make you feel like we've taken it too far?" I hold my hand up, blinded by the glittering orb.

"Nah. Wanna know the truth?"

"I'm not sure we know what that word means anymore."

He smirks. "Think what you want."

That inscrutable look in his eyes. I'm toast. But that's only because despite the insanity of it all, it *feels* incredible. I want to jump into his arms and start our engagement right. Data people don't trust feelings. Feelings change, and most dangerously, they can't always be trusted. But right now, they're fighting stronger than the data. In fact, they are punching the data flat on its back.

"I will" is all I manage to say, my brow knitted in a way that's giving away more than I would like. I consciously will it to smooth out.

He smiles at this like he can see right through me. Which is ridiculous.

However, I feel like I can see through him at this moment

too. He wants me to feel close to him, to lean on him even. And he hasn't taken this fake engagement lightly. I don't know why, or what he hopes it accomplishes—because it's more than 'in for a penny, in for a pound,' but his intentions come from respect, honor, care. It's coming across loud and clear from those piercing blue eyes.

"Are we crazy?" I ask.

"Honestly?" he says.

I nod.

"Absolutely."

I smile.

"But don't tell me you're not having an unexpected amount of fun too."

I nod.

His crinkles deepen. I love being the cause of that. Never had feelings about a crinkle one way or another, now they top all my lists. It's my turn to lean in and hug him. I nuzzle in and kiss him on the cord of his strong neck. It feels like the most natural thing in the world.

He turns my head and kisses me back. It feels endless and sensual, and layered with all the things we shared.

"Hear me out," he says when we've parted—just in time for Jim to return to the tasting room. "Just for today, what if we let ourselves stop playing around like this isn't the real thing? Not to other people like we've been doing, but to ourselves. That kiss we just shared, for instance. Are you telling me you didn't feel something? That it didn't bring you back to everything we've done and knock you for a loop?"

I open my mouth to answer, but he places a finger at my lips.

"No, no, no. Let's not overcomplicate it by talking about it. Just *feel*. Like we did the other night, like our bodies are telling us to do right now." He quirks a brow.

I know what he's getting at. And, yes, it would be a relief after the seriousness and the raised stakes of today. A vacation from this mess that I've made of my life. I'm quite good at compartmentalizing. When you know the stats are that you have a decent chance of not making it to your twelfth birthday, you learn to live in the moment.

"Okay, well, where are we off to then, my betrothed?"

He squints. "That doesn't feel like you're taking it seriously."

"What?" I raise my palms.

"Who says 'betrothed'?"

I move close, so I can see my reflection in his eyes. I lace my hand through his hair. I see him try not to react.

"Your fiancée does. The one who's madly in love with you, has been since the moment we met." I kiss him. Then I look at him in a way that can mean I am one hundred percent serious, or believe I am. Then I smile huge, just to put him off balance, present the possibility I could just be an Oscar-caliber actress. There. Now, I can get into this. It's *fun*.

And after all those years of following the rules just to survive, breaking them is mind-blowing, more of a culture shock than leaving Manhattan behind for Sydney. And who says it's wrong? Because hearing what Aiden said before—about my parents' reaction if they knew my entire life is a farce for their protection—shifted my perspective on that from mildly amusing to starkly disturbing. I've fucked up. And I'm unhappy. And they'd rather help me than know I'm struggling to keep up appearances all alone. I'm damned if I do, damned if I don't.

Something else he said comes to mind: *in for a penny, in for a pound*. I chose this path. And those untrustworthy feelings tell me there's much more hope along this road where I'm feeling alive and sexy and cared-for and fake-but-potently loved. I'd be an idiot not to see where it goes. It's certainly got much more promise than confessing to my parents that my life's a mess at this moment.

Besides, something deep inside keeps asking me: *is it?* Because looking in his eyes, feeling his strong arm pulling me close, the strength of his chest against me, feels off-the-charts incredible.

"Okay, betrothed. Ready for some more wine? Let's hit another vineyard."

TWENTY-SEVEN

AIDEN

Oh, did we ever hit the vino. Best day of my life, hands down. Six hours of wine tasting, groping, playing the newly-engaged card, enjoying the special treatment of those desperate to experience the kind of love we are emanating by the bucketful.

You'd have to be one blind motherfucker not to see the spark between us. Since we left old Jimbo's vineyard, we've been connected at all times. Fingers gliding over skin, my arms pulling her near, her body molding to mine as she lets me closer and closer—both physically and emotionally.

The idea of pulling away from her is impossible. Because something has softened in her since her confession and it makes her even more beautiful. And that she chose me to put her trust in has taken me to dizzying heights.

Sure, the alcohol had removed a lot of the logical hurdles we'd probably be jumping otherwise, but the truth is, we both need it. She's so hard on herself, and me? Well, I have never done intimacy. Playing it, shit I can do that. I know what women want. Or I *knew*. And none of it had to do with authenticity before. But this does. And that scares the ever-loving hell out of me. Enter adult grape juice, stage left. And things get a hell of a lot easier.

If I didn't know better, I'd say this Aiden has some better character traits than the one formerly known as the genuine article. He's certainly enjoying himself more. And the chemistry bubbling away?

Well, six hours of caresses, stolen feels below a pants' waist, standing so that my cock is against her ass in a way that shows her exactly what we're doing later? Bring out all your PPE, because as we key our way into the presidential suite, the elements are in place for one major explosion.

Show her this is real, I think, but it's unnecessary, because my body's already instinctively on the task. I lift her and back her against the door. My lips are on hers and desire takes over. My tongue is in and just the idea of this makes me grind against her. She's on the level because she groans into my mouth and this makes my tongue plunge deeper.

She pushes on the back of my head, opening wider to let me in, her lower half also getting the message as she spreads her legs to let me in deeper, squeezes her thighs around me tighter. My heart beats so fast, I can't think straight. I need to remove these clothes between us.

Gently, I lower her to her feet and for the second time today, get down on my knees. This time I remove her shoes, unhook her pants, lower her zipper, slide her pants down and off. I kiss the inside of her ankle and work my way up, my tongue trailing hungrily, driving her wild, I can tell from the way she's squirming and working her legs wider to let me in where she wants.

I spend my time at her thigh, enjoying the sweet torture I'm delivering. And then, with no warning, I slip my tongue between the lips of her beautiful pussy. She shudders, her breath catches. Her hands tangle in my hair and tug.

I do it again, this time slower, working my way from the bud of her clit to her opening, then I thrust. I want in. And from her reaction, the yank on my hair, she wants it too. In and in and in. God, she tastes like heaven. Then I use my hands to pull her apart and lap and lap until she's trembling so much she's going to fall.

"Come for me, my love," I say. Am I playing with that word? I don't know. In this moment, I truly don't. Nothing seems to matter except the way we feel. And what is wrong with that? We feel amazing. Together. We make each other feel amazing. And I'm going to enjoy feeling her come on my mouth. I pull back and layer the lightest licks over and over on her nub, on the sensitive skin of her pussy lips and in seconds, she's pulsing around me, over the edge, crashing into the oblivion of orgasm.

She screams out. She clenches, then goes to jelly.

"Oh, but I haven't finished with you yet, Olivia, my love. You're never going to forget the night you got engaged." I pick her up again. All I want to do is care for her, hold her in my arms. *Olivia, Olivia.* What has she done to me?

I take her to the bed and peel my clothes off. *Yes, I notice the way you notice my chest, love. I see the way your eyes move to my cock, betrothed.* And I fucking love it. It's what makes me pull you into my arms, and kiss you, the taste of your sweet pussy on my tongue now on yours.

And you like it, you erotic little wonder, you. You moan and your lapping picks up a frenetic pace. You want more. Well, I'm going to give it to you, you fucking beautiful woman. You might be taking a risk with a bad boy, but at least you get the experienced lover that comes with it. And there isn't a woman in the world who's brought me to the level of desperation I am at to be inside you.

God help you, you make it worse. You slip out from beneath me. You're drunk and wanting to get wild now, too, bold in the wake of your crushing orgasm. You kneel alongside the bed, pull me to the edge, push yourself between my legs and take my cock —the length of it—all the way down your throat.

The growl that comes from my throat scares me. It's the physical equivalent of the emotional O.D. I've been riding these past days, and I twist my fists in your golden locks and push you to the rhythm of my cock, riding your mouth in the purest bliss.

Then I raise your head, and you wipe your lip like the perfect good girl but slut for me that every man wants just for himself. You've done this before, and I don't want to think about that now. All I want is to switch spots with you, bend you over and let you feel that cock fill you to the hilt. And within seconds of sliding into your slippery, tight pussy, we're both bashing into each other uncontrollably.

I reach around and feel your full, firm tits, pinch that nipple until you call out, and then we're shuddering toward another world-destroying orgasm. Me and you, betrothed. Let the rest of the world burn around us. And I kiss and hold you so tightly after, making sure you understand this is precisely how I feel.

TWENTY-EIGHT

OLIVIA

I wish I could say I wake the next morning to my new life, the love expressed between us, the goalposts we shifted back again and again having brought us to a place of security, where the fake was definitely behind us and the real was undeniable.

But the second I open my eyes—with a wicked hangover, nonetheless—and I see drop-dead-gorgeous sleeping Aiden with his hand possessively gripping my hip, I'm spiraling in a cyclone of doubt.

The feelings and the fiery meeting of our bodies were the genuine article, proof that our faking had turned into the real thing. There's no denying that, but getting engaged to someone I barely know? Well, that move is planted firmly in the fake camp. That's a gesture for the world to see. It's insurance against our lies. How could I have even entertained for a second the idea that it's anything but? I know how—his words and actions, his lovemaking say this is as real as it gets.

You need to keep your wits about you. But then he opens his eyes and the crinkles around them work their magic, and his smile lights up his whole face, and he dips his chin as if to say, *yes, this smile is all you,* I'm putty.

"Come here, beautiful," he says. He pulls me in, nuzzles his cheek and nose at the side of my face, my neck. Then he repositions so we're face to face, noses nearly touching. His lips press against mine, softly. I watch his eyes close like he's savoring the feel of our connection the same way I am. Then his kiss goes molten, possessed. Hands, hips, legs, all finding their rightful places against each other's bodies.

That electric heat obliterates any chance of me keeping my senses.

Then he ends the kiss with a last nibble on my lower lip. "Pop quiz," he says.

I arch a brow.

"Was that kiss real or fake?"

I feel my muscles instantly tense. What is he playing?

I open my mouth to say, well, I'm not exactly sure what, but something to the effect of *what the fuck?* when he goes back in, this time kissing me more fiercely, overtaking me in a way I am desperately eager to be overtaken. Who knew that a woman with a lifetime of trying to maintain control would so deeply want to be dominated and forced into the unknown in this way? It feels so incredibly *liberating*.

Then he moves south, kissing my neck, my chest, then cupping my breast and sucking at the nipple. I cry out.

He stops, his fingers taking over where his mouth had been.

"Real? Or fake?" He's smiling in a way I couldn't read if I had all the magical powers on Earth.

"Ai—"

He stops me with a finger to my mouth. And that's when I realize I'm not being dominated, because it doesn't feel like he's one entity and I'm the other. It's like we're two parts that have at long last come together. And the part that he holds knows exactly what the part I hold needs.

As if to prove my theory, he parts my knees and traces a

finger expertly toward my thigh, tickling, turning my skin to gooseflesh, then feathering his fingers around the edges of my opening. Then he slips inside my soaked folds and applies the perfect amount of pressure, slicking his finger around in the most heavenly way. I'm already close to coming when he turns onto his back and pulls me on top of him.

I feel the stiffness of him against my spread lips. I'm pulsing, hungry to feel him inside me.

"Real or fake?" I say this time, despite myself, getting into the mysterious eroticism of it. "Fake," I answer for him, sliding back and forth onto his shaft.

"Real," he says.

"Real," I say.

"Fake." He grinds against me, then reaches for a condom, tears the packet with his teeth and rearranges so he can roll it down his impressive cock.

He lifts me by the hips and lowers me onto him.

"Real," he whispers, as he pulls my face down to his, kisses me, his tongue and cock thrusting in a rhythm that threatens to shatter me. Is it the game he's playing? Or has he said this last word at this moment of our connection because he means it?

I sit up and enjoy his eyes on me as I ride him, my hips grinding, swinging. He anchors my waist with his big, strong hands and pushes up into me harder, deeper.

I've never felt sexier, and further proof of my two-parts-uniting theory, I've never felt more powerful. I can see the results in the lusty look on his face.

He pulls me down tighter, we both rock deeper, my knees go tingly, cold, the climax inching its way closer, closer.

"Look at you fucking me," he says. "If the way I feel so deep inside you, your tight little cunt just for me, taking every bit of me, isn't the genuine article, then nothing is. You. Feel. So. Good."

He pushes me with trembling, clenching hands in one final thrust and I'm clenching and pulsing around him in an orgasm that rocks me in white-hot electricity from head to toe. Feeling his hot liquid shoot inside the condom makes the orgasm echo, the shot of ecstasy hitting me again and again.

I collapse against him, and he gathers me in his arms, still inside me. He rakes my hair from my face and presses soft, loving kisses along the apples of my cheeks.

It's either the realest moment of happiness in my life, or the beginning of the end for me. Because no one will ever compare to Aiden.

THE REST of the company left yesterday, so when we head down for some breakfast in the half-full dining room, there are only strangers. A couple of women give Aiden the double-take. He's famous and movie-star handsome, so it makes sense, but I'm not sure I'll get used to it.

I find I'm ravenous, and the scrummy Middle Eastern breakfast I've ordered—a colorful plate of poached eggs, smoky beans, Israeli salad, hummus and pita—is just what the doctor ordered.

Aiden looks down at his standard bacon and scrambled eggs with toast and pulls a boyish grimace.

"Order envy?" I say, glowing from my multiple orgasms, undeniable connection, and expert ability to compartmentalize the gnawing concern that this bliss will come crashing down around me.

"Of course not," he says.

"Want to share?" I say, smirking, reaching for his hand, enjoying the way his eyes lock onto me when I do.

"Breakfast? Yes. You? Never."

He looks delectable tucking into my eggs as I reach out my

fork for him to open up and take a bite. Oh, does this echo through my white-hot core.

"More?" I say.

"Yes," he growls. Each bite grows increasingly wolfish. He licks his lips and I might need to drag him back to bed.

I'm just thinking I need to slow down when my phone rings.

His brows bounce. Is he jealous?

"Who's calling you during feeding time?"

I glance down. It's my mother. I press the side button to ignore the call. I'm certainly not speaking to her in front of Aiden again.

I go back to my own food but find everything to do with mouths and forks is now erotic. Every morsel that slides down my throat is bliss. I enjoy watching him enjoy my pleasure.

"Olivia," he says. Then he lowers his voice, leans closer, whispers. "What are you doing to me?"

We sit there, in the dense air of this question we're both enraptured in this high.

My phone trills again. Mom. Excellent timing.

Aiden's eyes dart to the screen.

"Maybe she needs you."

I press the ignore button again, now getting a bit worried. She's not a multiple caller. Doesn't even leave messages. Just figures I'll call when I get around to it. Inside she'll be frantic until I ring back, but she'll never let me know it. I guess we have that in common.

Then a text message alert pings. Again, we both see it. "You're engaged to someone else???????? Does Corey know?"

I screw my eyes shut. How adult of me! That will surely make this go away!

"What is it?" he asks.

I turn the screen his way so he can read her words.

"Call her," he says.

"No. What am I going to say?" I let my fork drop with a clatter to the plate. From the periphery, I see a few heads turn. I should never have put that ring on. What was I thinking? Now I've taken this to the point of no return. How can I make this right?

I can see it right now: *Sorry, Mom! Not only did it not work out with Corey, but I've signed myself up for a fake engagement with a Romeo who's bedded more women than Hugh Hefner.*

Or I can go on pretending it's real and then we can start planning a wedding that's never going to happen. At what point do I drop the bomb that the wedding's off? No rehearsal dinner or limo to the church?

Yeah, this was definitely a great way to save Mom from worry. Excellent job, Olivia!

His hand squeezes mine. "You in there?"

"No," I say.

He laughs. "Well, at least you haven't lost your sense of humor."

I open my eyes, flash a sheepish smile. He does make me feel like I'm not in this alone. And that is a comfort I'm unused to indulging in.

"Hey, we've got this."

"How?" I say. My voice is kind, my hands are clenching his back. I want him to know I appreciate it, and even though I want to blame all of this on him, I know it took both of us to get to this point. Even now, I'm not sure I would go back and do things differently. My life is unrecognizable from what it was before I got myself into this—brighter, bigger.

"If I have to take this all the way down the aisle, through a couple of pregnancies and births, some over-the-top Christmases and ponies for the eighth birthday, then I'll do it. You know that. In fact, nothing would make me happier."

I'm sure my shock over his statement is evident. My eyes have bulged so intensely, I can barely see.

"Aiden, don't say things like that."

"Why?"

"Because this isn't the way fake relationships go."

"Isn't it? I didn't get my rulebook." His eyes are kind, but his mouth is tight, serious.

"If we keep taking it further, how will we ever extricate ourselves?" I feel my strength drain from me.

"You can extricate yourself anytime you want, beautiful."

"I know that," I say, a bit too indignantly. What happened to us being real? I want to ask it, but for some reason I can't. It suddenly feels like too much is at stake—namely, everything.

"And the reason you haven't is because you care about me."

"So? You care about *me*."

"Can't deny that, gorgeous."

"So, what are you saying?"

"I'm saying things have taken an unexpected turn. You're the data girl. Based on the evidence, what's the best course of action?"

Did I believe he would do anything but speak in the infuriating riddles he's been lashing me with all along?

TWENTY-NINE

AIDEN

She's got to get there herself. That much is clear. Every time we get too close to what's really between us, she pulls back. She's afraid of hurting her parents, but there's more. And I'm going to have to keep playing along until she tells me. Is it ironic that the one time I don't feel like playing games, that's exactly what I have to do? Fuck yes. But whatever it takes, however long it takes, I'm doing it for a future with this woman. She's worth it.

Still, it's tense as we pack up our things in the room. "I'll give you some time if you want to ring your mum," I say, not waiting for an answer. "I'll be in the business lounge. Take your time."

No sooner do I have my laptop logged onto the Wi-Fi than my brother Finn sees me online and rings in for a video chat. I'm glad it's him and not Dad because maybe he can prime me for what I might be facing. Dad often calls Finn when he wants the truth about things where I'm considered. But I'd hope that after our talk yesterday that he'd come to me directly.

In contrast to my sordid reputation, Finn's a proper bloke—didn't want to go into Dad's line of business, and to prove his path worthy, made himself a cool million on his own by the time he was eighteen with a surf brand empire which is now a multi-billion-dollar international label.

He's got a shit-eating grin and he's shaking his head like I've done it again. "Brother, you've done it this time. Engaged! To a girl I've never even met. I'm sure this won't go down in flames."

I've been sort of putting out the idea that I had a secret woman all this time since Dad and I had a talk about my history with women and the casual barbs led to me pledging—without any coaxing from Dad—that I'd be serious with a woman by this year's conference.

I'm pretty sure no one was buying it, but I knew it would give me the fake relationship fallback plan if we got to the date and I had nothing else lined up. I feel awful at the idea of Olivia having any part in that, but I barely recognize the guy I was when these thoughts stacked up to something logical.

None of it makes sense now. I'm gonna have to be out with this at some point because I don't want any of this ugliness mucking up the purity of our relationship.

"Yup, took the plunge," I say, with no emotion. Can't sully Olivia in any way, better to keep mum.

"I don't know what you're up to, but I need to meet this woman. And not just because Dad wants my feedback on this secret engagement that has blown up all over the news today."

After my talk with Dad, I presume Finn is putting more importance on Dad's asking for his opinion than is true. But after years of that family dynamic, I can't blame Finn for taking this on. I don't worry about it. Olivia will knock his socks off.

"I need to see this lady for myself, because Dad seems to be smitten with her. So much so, that he's not even half as angry about the bombshell as I would have thought."

Now my smile gives me away. Thinking about Olivia and the positive changes she's brought to my life will do that.

"Aha, I see how it is."

"Fuck you," I say.

He laughs, raises his palms. "It's good to see you like this, Aiden. Never thought I'd see the day."

I don't say anything.

"So, I'll see you in an hour at Ridgeview Vineyard. You know the restaurant? They've just started carrying a co-branded wine with our logo on it. That's Missy for you. She sorted the whole deal. It's biodynamic, bottled in recycled glass, saves the red pandas, all that shit."

"I don't know." Who knows how Olivia is going to feel after the conversation with her mum? "I have to check with Olivia first."

"Check with me on *what?*" I have to hand it to her, she does an excellent job getting back at me for sneaking up on her call yesterday. I try to keep my face neutral, though the sight of her turns the room's wattage up about a million volts.

Olivia makes her way around the desk and behind me, bending down to get her face in the camera. She flashes him that killer smile. There's a stiffness to her, but he wouldn't know that the way I do. I lay a protective palm at the small of her back.

"The famous Olivia! My soon-to-be sister-in-law! You up to meet with my wife and me for lunch? I can't believe Aiden's been keeping you all to himself."

She turns to look at me, and there's tumult there—a deep connection, but fear, and stress that I put there, placing her in a conundrum where lying is the only road. I want to make it better. I will make it better. I pull her onto my lap, and if I didn't know better, I'd say she's instantly a bit relieved as I pull her into my embrace.

"I'd love to meet you and your wife. Your brother has been quite selfish, hasn't he? A bit of a dark horse, he is. But you can fill me in on all of that later."

"She's got your number, Ay. I love her already."

"Everyone does," I say, my eyes glued to hers, so she'll know I mean it.

"Great. It's a date."

WE RING off but I don't let Olivia go.

"How did it go with your mother?" Our hands our caressing, fingers entwined, exploring every plane is bliss.

"Oh, you don't want to know about that."

"Come on, Olivia. Don't do that. I fucked up with the ring, I want to help you. But first I need to know what we're dealing with."

"First of all, it's just as much my fault as it is yours. Probably more. I didn't have to agree, did I?" She's yelling a bit, certainly more frantic than I've seen her.

"Maybe you did."

I can see as soon as the words are out that she's not ready for the truth at the moment. I feel like the human embodiment of that bared teeth emoji. Well done, Aiden. Took you all of two minutes to push her too far. So much for giving her the space to feel comfortable on her own.

Just as I thought, this new rush of hurried pressure has only made her shut down further on the possibility of taking things seriously. Or at least of allowing herself to give into the way she feels. Hence the cool cucumber losing her shit.

"You're sexy when you lose it."

She cocks her head and shoots me the stink eye. "Do not go there."

"Then tell me what your mother said."

"No. Let's go to lunch and torture you a little bit with your brother and then I'll see if that makes me feel like I want to share with you later."

"Deal," I say, standing and lifting her, and sweeping her hair from her neck. I smile at her. I am so simply happy in this moment, I cannot help but wrap her in my arms and hold her tightly. By the time we disentangle, she looks calmer. At least her eye isn't twitching the way it was when I left the room to come down here.

I can feel the power of the impact our connection has on her. And I only know this because it's exactly the one she has on me. I recognize that look in her eye. I've been seeing it in the mirror all week.

The one that says it's pointless trying to fight this, the one that's a mix of the greatest relief and joy and the sheer terror that tells you to resist and protect yourself at any cost because this much bliss cannot be real . . . despite how many times you've been swept up in the intensity of it all, and despite the fact that at this moment, you've one hundred percent convinced yourself it is.

"BROTHER!" Finn and I share the same blue eyes, but he's got darker features and a shit ton of facial hair. He always has a scruffy cut to his hair and there have been no end to the stereotypes the tabloids have used to distinguish the two of us: City Brother versus Beach Brother, Sydney's Most Wicked Billionaire Playboy and His Soft-Hearted Brother.

It's good to see him and I'm sure my hug lets him know that.

"Milly's rearranging the shop's display. Don't ask." He rolls his eyes but it's clear how proud and enamored he is. They've been strong since grade eight. I don't know how he did it then, and I still don't. But he's told me he's a one-woman kind of guy and I'm pretty sure growing up in the angry shards of our parents' disintegrating marriage had something to do with his take on that.

The fact that I've gone in the opposite direction is a mystery for the experts. Regardless, Finn's a stand-up guy, never a bad word to say about anyone.

Except me, if I deserve it. We've always been frank with each other and had each other's backs. When it comes to my reputation with the ladies, he's certainly been ashamed of me more than once. And not in the way my dad can be, where it's all about reputation. Instead, Finn's always saying, "You're better than this," though there were several times that was probably hard for him to say.

"Finn, meet Olivia Barker, my fiancée."

He smiles ear to ear, looks at Olivia with a huge grin, then embraces her in a hug. "Welcome to the family," he says. I can tell she's surprised. He's so different than me. The openness and warmth he emanates is right up her alley. Wouldn't be surprised if she's already thinking she chose the wrong brother. I couldn't blame her. But I will do everything in my power to be the man she deserves, because at this moment, there isn't a thing in the world that matters more.

"It's so great to meet you," she says, looking from Finn to me and back again in a way that feels like she really is literally becoming a part of us.

"My incredible pleasure, Olivia. I've been waiting for the day when I finally get to meet the woman who can tame Aiden. And I'm guessing from the investment he made in that rock, which could have financially backed a small island nation, that you've managed it."

Hang on. That's sarcasm. He doesn't believe this. Why does that piss me off so bloody much when so much of this has been a pack of lies? *Because it's the real deal and you know it.*

"It has not been easy, let me tell you," she says, warmth and instant familiarity in her voice. She squeezes my hand, and I can't help but stare at her. We *are* in this together. There's no denying that.

"As if you're a simple woman," I say, surprising myself with being so forthright. I tell myself I didn't get caught up in the sensations set off by her touch, but that it's just a way to show we're the real deal—airing our peccadillos like an old married couple.

"I'm sure she's anything but. Why don't we sit down and I can find out for myself?"

"Aiden!" Milly yells just as I pull out Olivia's chair from the table. "Congratulations!"

She sticks her arms out for Olivia to embrace her, just like Finn did. God, those two are something else. I was never jealous of what they had, but now I wonder why I wasn't. *Because you didn't want it until you met Olivia.*

"We're going to have so much fun planning the wedding!" Milly says when she extricates herself. "And it will be so great to have some estrogen around for once. These Wheatley brothers, God! Your new mother-in-law, well, she's a bit of a handful, but you can't blame her. What their dad did to her! You just have to be very gentle with her and never talk about any problems, then she'll be absolutely fine. But don't worry. You can talk to me."

I can see Olivia is overwhelmed by Milly's giant personality. Most people are. I, myself, usually button right up because she speaks enough for the whole group. It exhausts me. But she's so kind, thoughtful, and supportive that you have to forgive her overzealousness.

She calms down after a few days, so there's that. My brother says it has to do with her being an orphan as a child, so he sees it as a gift he's giving her, letting her shine when no one cared to give her a second glance before. And every time I think of that, I am reminded what a beautiful soul my brother has and how fucking much he loves his wife.

THIRTY

AIDEN

"So, who's going to tell me the story of how you guys met?" Finn says.

"You know what, I'll take this one," Olivia says. She bulges her eyes, like we should ready ourselves for the tale. "I'd just come here from America and I'd followed someone who probably would have been best not followed."

She's got the attention of Milly and Finn.

"It turned out the second he was alone in our apartment, he was *schtoinking* someone else."

I could see their eyes bulge and I'm really surprised she came out and said that. These are people she doesn't know. She doesn't need to tell them any of that and yet here she is making herself vulnerable and honest, and I really admire it. Is this forthrightness an extension of the honesty she's entrusted me with? I hope so.

She looks absolutely stunning. She squeezes my hand and I take it as a sign that I've got this correct. I inch closer to her.

"His loss," I say.

"He always says that," Olivia says, and I absolutely love the way she does, as if she and I really do have this intimacy, this history, and the look she shares with me says that. How can our lies feel closer to the truth than anything else ever has?

I reach for her hand under the table, not on top where every-body can see and she doesn't look back at me, but she smiles, and that smile is for me. She's coming around. I notice she didn't use the swimming pool story we made up. Instead, she tells them how a woman threw her drink on me at the Grand Hotel. Of course, she doesn't say it was last week, but that's a minor detail as far as I'm concerned. I could have met her yesterday and I'd still know she was the woman for me.

Milly is full of questions and Finn is observing in the silent, casual way he does when he's making his mind up about something.

"SO, HOW DID HE PROPOSE?" Milly picks up Olivia's hand to inspect the rock, the chunk of me she's carrying around with her, to my utter honor.

"Well, he got down on one knee like a proper romantic and made sure to fill me up with some wine beforehand. And with the most genuine expression on his face, asked if he could put that ring on my finger."

She didn't mention the words exchanged. *Fake* probably wouldn't have translated well. In for a penny, in for a pound, is something else I remember saying. Probably not my strongest moment.

Still, hearing it from her is incredible.

"Well, I for one am super excited," Milly says. "This guy, you know, he's never once introduced any of those girls of his to us. And there have been *a lot*."

Does Olivia realize she's dug her nails into my palm? My lip quirks. I'm sure she's clocking my reaction. It's good to see her jealousy. I feel my body responding, keen to show her she's got nothing to worry about, that every bit of me belongs to her.

"Yeah, why would I?" I say. "I mean, none of them were worth it. None of them were going to be sticking around."

Milly shakes her head. A huge grin spreading.

Finally, Finn speaks up. "I still can't believe it. Is this for real? It doesn't seem like it can be."

"Do you even have to ask? Look at him. I barely even recognize him," Milly says.

"Yeah, but you're a romantic. You read in all the stuff you want to read. I'm a realist." He turns to me. "How do I know that you're not just doing this to make Dad happy?"

I could punch him for making me look like a weenie in front of Olivia, but that would make me look like an even bigger weenie. Instead, I rearrange my posture, tug at my shirtsleeves. "Have I ever done anything just to make Dad happy?"

"You've certainly tried to maintain an appearance that you're doing things that would make him happy." Which is, if we're being completely honest here, what got me to a place where I met Olivia, where I felt like I could present her with this half-baked plan.

I hadn't even been honest with myself about my motivations, which were always to get to know her. If I pleased Dad along the way? Sure, that would be a bonus. But nothing—from the moment I saw her—meant more to me than bringing Olivia into my world, making her my world. So, if it took me so long to admit that to myself, then why was I getting so angry at Finn for suspecting things weren't the way we described?

"Look, I don't have to prove anything to you," I say.

"All right, let's not all get angry at each other. It's just, it's kind of crazy. Have you seen the papers? It's like nobody believes it."

"Well, fuck them."

I see Olivia wince.

Again, her eyes go wide. I don't know what to do. *Say sorry, dick.* But I have never been much good at that, especially where my reputation is concerned, because I've never understood why it's anyone else's business. Lunch was making me realize that there are some things about me that I really feel ashamed to let Olivia know. "Sorry," I say to a few raised brows. *Yes, I'm a changed man.*

Sure, she probably Googled me already, but that narrative is not mine. Coming from me, it's something else altogether. And in that moment, I realize I owe her that ugly truth. If she's given me hers, it's the least I can do.

It's the second time in twenty-four hours I've yearned to be out with every ugly bit of my story to Olivia. As if I needed even more evidence that this was something special.

It's silent and awkward in the absence of my apology.

"So, then tell me about you," Olivia says. The fact that she's on my side here even when I've not given her much reason to be gives me a strength that soars through me. "Aiden said you built the most amazing company and that Milly is a huge part of that. I mean you guys are just living the dream. That's amazing. How did it all come about?"

Finn looks from Olivia to me, then back again, as if deciding to let it drop. He's not a man who leaves things unsaid. It's the thing I most respect about him. But he's giving me space, and for that I'm grateful. I don't think it's possible to be in a room with Olivia and me and not feel our connection. This is something that cannot lie.

Finn leans his upper body over the table, elbows relaxed, hands clasped. "From the very beginning of the time I spent at Dad's office, I knew I could not be happy like that. I felt like a caged animal every single day I went in there. I also knew that if I didn't want to do it, I was going to have to prove to him that I could make a profitable business that would make me happy, something great.

"That's how it started. He didn't think I could do it, but quickly I realized it didn't really matter. I stopped worrying about him and started doing it for myself and the right reasons, and then for Milly, and it just took off."

Despite our differences, there's so much in his story, in his motivations that shines a light on my own, and I'm sure Olivia has taken note.

"That's awesome," Olivia says. "How many people have a dream and just go off and make it happen?"

"Tell us about you. What do you do at P.I.C., Olivia?"

"I'm a data scientist, and I know that's not quite as sexy as living out the romantic surf empire dream, but—"

I cut her off. "It's amazing, what she's done. She can even make you guys more money. Her area of expertise is where the whole future is. Anyone can look at a sheet of numbers, but you have to know what to do with it. Someone like Olivia does, and she's one in a million."

Something in Finn softens. "I just wish we had known about you, Olivia."

"Well, now you do," I say. "I'm very lucky to have her. I probably don't deserve her."

"That's for sure," Finn says in a way that makes everyone at the table squirm, and makes me want to punch him a little. But only because he's right.

By the time we leave the lunch, Milly's already got Olivia's phone number. She's making her promise to meet up with her and talk about what they might need for the wedding and gushing about how they're going to be buddies.

Again, I'm not surprised, and yet I leave with a strange feeling. Those things that I felt ashamed of, I need to talk to Olivia about them because I don't want to be that man anymore.

THIRTY-ONE
OLIVIA

I loved feeling his hand on mine under the table as I got to know Finn and Milly. It would be so easy to pretend this was my real life, just lose myself in enjoying it. In fact, I got so caught up in trying to prove the authenticity of the whole thing, for a minute there I believed it was just a regular old meeting, and I say so to Aiden in the car.

"What's a *regular old meeting?*" he says. "You think most people just meet, fall in love, and *boom*, happily ever after? If that was the case, the world would be a whole different place for men."

"Sure, but—"

"There's something special between us, beautiful." I look at him. He's speaking directly and that's so unlike him. "I'm sure I'm throwing you off," he says. We're at the car and he laces his hands through mine. "But the truth is . . . you and me, don't deny there wasn't something there the first night.

"The more I get to know you, the more I realize you're not the kind of girl who would let a stranger kiss her on day one, especially one who proposed the kind of crap I did. You got something to tell me?"

I'm too terrified to answer. Everything has just suddenly gone so high stakes. I just look at my ring, look at him and smile and hope he'll let it go.

He studies me, our eyes darting back and forth. *Okay, yes, love is on my mind. But there isn't a way in this world I'm going there.* And yet, I want so badly to toss that caution to the wind and speak the words he's asking to hear. He's one infuriating guy, but that's only because I care what he thinks.

And so, my words are a shock to my ears. "So, when are we finished with this?" I say. And I'm not sure why because it just seems like I'm trying to sabotage what should be a once-in-a-life-time moment.

"Well, what do the facts tell you?" he says.

I need to answer. This is the moment where I show him I'm in. I feel tears well up but there is no way in hell I'm letting them loose.

We let the silence hang there. There are things that need to be said, but neither of us are stepping up to say them. Aiden is putting this on me and I understand why. He's said so much, met me more than halfway, he's just confessed his love, and I'm standing paralyzed.

Until his shoulders sag, he pulls my knuckles to his lips, places a kiss that pulses right through me, then gently lowers my hands to my thighs, and ever so slowly slips his from mine. Look at him encouraging me, meeting me halfway.

I shiver and open my mouth with a pop his eyes stare at. But the words I want to say won't come out.

To make things worse, when we fly back, I decide I'm going back to my place. I say it before he can ask. I tell myself it's just a bit of time I need, to get up the courage to go all in.

"I think you need some space," I say instead. "I see what's happening." *What the fuck did I mean by that?*

His reaction is nil, as it should be. I can't tell if he feels angry, relieved that someone's finally put the brakes on this runaway train, or if he couldn't give a shit because he's finally had it with my lack of faith.

So, if he's not curious about "what's happening" then why am I still talking? And yet, I am. There's sabotage written all over this, and I wish I could explain why. "You didn't like those things your brother was saying about you. You *want* to be that man you've been with me these past few days, and so you're throwing yourself into the relationship that makes this behavior come easy to you. But what are you going to do when these feelings wear away?"

"It sounds like you want that to happen," he says, and I can't blame him.

So why do I keep saying these things?

"You know, Olivia, I have tried every way to show you how I feel about you. I'm starting to feel like maybe you're just saying those things because that's what you want."

"Aiden, I—" I shake my head, but I can't speak. I don't know how to put this reticence into words. That anger tight at his jaw has my name all over it. And I want more than anything to make it disappear.

"I think I do need some space," he says, that inscrutable look still etched on his features.

When his driver stops in front of my building, I swear I don't even recognize the place. It's not like it's been much of a home to me. In fact, the strongest connection I've had isn't in there, or anyplace I've ever called home, but with Aiden. So why am I making him leave? I want to just say, "Never mind, I want to be with you!" But I can't. I'm being pulled in so many directions.

It's so dangerous, these feelings I have. I'm already dreading his driving away and the sinking feeling I will have in my heart. Am I doing this because I'm so used to shrinking into my own shell that I can't do anything else, or am I testing this, seeing what happens when we're pushed?

He walks me to my door. "Olivia, you're right. I don't like the man my brother sees when he looks at me—or the one my father sees. And that was my original motivation for wanting to find the right woman for the job. And boy, that worked like a charm. Those men have *never* had such respect in their eyes when they looked at me. But I couldn't enjoy it, because I've been lying to you. There was never an ultimatum."

I startle as he lowers my bag to the ground. "What? I don't understand."

"Here's the truth, gorgeous. I felt it, just like you did, from that very first moment. And this conference represented the perfect opportunity to get to know you as quickly and urgently as I felt like I needed to. Juvenile? Yes. But come on, if I'd confessed my feelings and said, *hey, spend every waking minute with me and tell me everything that makes you tick, grace my family with your presence, show the world you're mine*, well, you'd say I was nuts and we certainly wouldn't have been able to enjoy the runaway passion we did.

"In fact, if you're being honest with yourself, gorgeous, you were never as free with me as you were in those hours when you convinced yourself you were pretending. Because you're just as scared as everyone is of getting used to feeling this kind of love, this kind of care, intimacy, passion, this kind of feeling like you want to be under each other's skin, and then having it snatched away."

And here I'd been preparing myself for the possibility that the whole game is off and that we're supposed to go back to being strangers pretending to be engaged. But his words, they undermine that preparation. That preparation was a bunch of shit. I look at him.

I want so badly to tell him he's right, to at least nod, so he knows I get it, that I understand what it took to say all that, that I forgive him for making up that ridiculous scenario, even though it's a lie—another lie. One which makes me feel quite stupid—but I can't. Isn't a lie one hurdle too many to overcome in all this?

I'm ruined for closeness. I can't do this to him, to myself. *What if? What if?* The question hangs over me like a trip wire. And on top of braving that—which I was ready to do, despite all the women he's had—now I need to find a way to trust a liar? Yes, I do. Because he's been so patient with me. And my omission about my health? Well, that wasn't exactly honesty in its purest form either, was it?

"I forgive you," I say. "And I didn't mean any of the things I said. I am scared of the intensity of my feelings. But I don't want to run from you. I won't. Everything you've done in this argument shows me that you want to meet me halfway, help me to put my trust in you, to lean on you. I don't blame you for getting angry. You were right. And I'm sorry."

His smile is one of the most beautiful sights I've ever seen. It goes all the way to his eyes. The crinkles are their deepest yet. I run my fingers there, then kiss him along there.

I trust him. And I realize that in trusting him, I have to trust him in *everything*. And if he says he's strong enough to love me no matter what, then I've got to let him do that. Otherwise this will never work.

"And I love you. And you know what that makes you, Aiden Wheatley?"

"The luckiest man in the world? The man who's just experienced the moment that should in all probability have been the one in which all was lost, and instead, found his beautiful, brave, woman saved it for him?"

. . .

GOD BLESS HIM, he leaves me with the world's hottest kiss and more comforting words. "You should have a bit of time here," he says. "Then you can remember how badly you need me and come right back to me."

I nod. "You're probably right. And thank you."

He looks around my apartment. "There isn't one bit of you in this place, is there?"

I trace his gaze around the living room, cold and sterile with its monotone color scheme and masculine furnishings.

"Not a thing," I say, "except you." I plant a kiss on his full lips, pull him in close from the nape. "Mmmm," I say when we've emerged from the hypnotic connection, everything dipped in the dew of our love.

"I'll probably see you in an hour," he says.

I shake my head, smiling. "Surely we can survive a night apart."

"You think?" he says.

It takes ages until we finally let each other go.

The door closing him outside my place echoes in my chest.

I listen to his footfalls down the stairs. When I can no longer hear them, I run to the window. I catch sight of his broad shoulders. Then he turns and looks at me with all the longing I feel.

I drop on my bed and let out a happy groan, splaying out on this bed that had been the cause of so much distress. It's the beginning of a new life.

I settle in for a long bath, close my eyes and try to make sense of everything. I'm bombarded with a sensory storm. Images of us talking, holding each other, laughing, it's all-consuming.

My head is spinning. I don't know which way is up. What I need is my best friend, Jolene. Luckily, we have the kind of time difference that would work in our favor at this hour. It's late here and early in New York. Jolene has always been my rock, the only thing that kept me from feeling like a total social outcast most of my life.

I mean, my days in the hospital could have been full of friends; we were all stuck there with nowhere to go and nothing to do, but nobody wants to give you attention over there. It's dangerous. Jolene, she always took the time to come to see me. When I missed a party, she'd bring me a cupcake or a party bag. She'd say it was from the host, but I'm sure more times than not, it was her bag.

We could sit there for hours on my tiny bed while she shared every bit of gossip, each detail I'd missed, so I would feel less left out. I'm lucky to have her.

"Hello!" She's so bright and happy. "I'm so glad to hear from you. How did your conference go?"

I'm not sure there are words to describe it. Good? Bad? I can't get a read on this, like uncharted territory, which would be amazing, because I'm pretty sure I've seen every kind of territory there is.

"Oh, Jolene, where do I begin?"

"Uh-oh, tell little Miss Jo everything. You know I can always find a solution no matter how crazy the problem."

"You do have a good track record, but this one's pretty much off the charts."

"Don't tell me you got back together with that idiot Corey?"

"Oh God, no." Yeah. We both had a good giggle about that.

"What is it then? Ooh, you met someone! And you slept with him!"

"What?!" I deny it, right away.

"My God, the girl who doesn't even have a twenty-date rule because she can't foresee the situation ever being right for sleeping with someone, so she doesn't make any rule at all? The girl who planned out the end of her virginity with a friend because otherwise she was never going to lose it? You're telling me *this girl*, since the five days I've spoken to you last, has met someone and had S-E-X?"

I cover my face in a pillow "Oh has she ever!" How can merely talking about him make me smile so hugely?

"I want every single detail. Who is he? Come on. I'll Google him right now. I've been on a Google hiatus. Jeremy had said we needed to be on one if we wanted our relationship to survive. So, I guess I *had* to. But you see? This is why the internet is vital! How did I miss this? Is he your friend on Facebook? Can I spy on him?" She's clicking away, clearly leaving the Google hiatus for dust.

"Isn't Jeremy going to be upset?"

"Jeremy Schmeremy. You had S-E-X with a stranger!"

"Okay then. Well, I'm not sure if he does Facebook, not personally anyway."

"Who'd you meet? Is he like Batman?"

"Yes, I'm dating Bruce Wayne. I'd let you know if he was Batman."

"What? You don't even like that. You make money for lots of people, but you think money corrupts and all that. You used to wear that T-shirt all the time: RICH PEOPLE SUCK. It's why nobody ever talked to you."

God, why do I talk so much? "I know, and listen, nobody's more shocked than me. But believe it or not, some of them don't suck. I was wrong. Now given my history, is it really gross for me to say that flying on a private jet is everything you would think it was and more?"

"Hold the phone. What did you just say?"

"We took his private jet to and from Hunter Valley, which probably would have taken an hour to drive to."

"Wait a minute. He *owns* a plane! Who is this guy? Give me his name right now."

"Aiden Wheatley."

"Wheatley, Wheatley...He's not one of those brothers that dated the pop singer?"

"No, you're thinking of the Hemsworths."

"Oh my God. I hate you. Okay, I need to get on a plane. When am I coming, and is there one for me?"

"What are you talking about? You have a boyfriend."

"Yes, but he's so boring, and he's not a millionaire."

"Actually, Aiden is a billionaire."

"Oh my God, we can't be friends anymore. Stop it." I'm finally going to bust. There's an unexpected prickle of heat at my eyes; they're happy tears. Telling Jo makes it feel real somehow. The words I'm saying are so unrecognizable as my life, it's no wonder I was having trouble walking that line between real and fake.

"Aiden Wheatley, here he is. I found him. Hang on...In line to inherit financial products company—what the heck is a financial products company anyway? P.I.C., second richest man in Australia, 100th richest man in the world. What happened? You couldn't break the top fifty?"

"Jolene, come on."

"No, no. You've been a wet blanket way too many times. You owe me this—especially after moving all the way across the world! Let's have some fun. Ooh, let's start looking at purses."

"Stop it."

"If you're not going to be any fun about it, what's the point?"

"Well, all right. What kind of purse would you—no, I can't be that kind of woman."

"You are so boring. *I* should have been the one to date a billionaire. It's so wasted on you. I—" She goes silent suddenly. "Hold on, hold the phone! There's a photo of you with Aiden Wheatley, and you're wearing an engagement ring that's the size of a child's head. This can't be right, because you wouldn't do this without telling your best friend. It says you are fucking engaged. This is not you. What the fuck is going on? Now I'm getting really scared. Are you sick again?"

"No, I'm not sick again. I know, it's very out of character for me. I understand that." I try to explain to her that first night and how we stumbled upon this plan. I leave out the truth of what Aiden confessed today—that none of that was true. I'm not sure why I don't admit this part. Is it because I feel too stupid, or because I think it paints him in a bad light? If I can't be honest in front of Jolene, I've got absolutely no hope. And here I am congratulating myself on this new level of openness I've achieved.

"Oh my God, how could you think that would make your parents happy? Why would you think they even *want* to be happy? Happy is for idiots."

"Stop. You've seen what my mom's been through."

"They don't want to just 'be happy.' They want your life to be fulfilling in a way that makes them happy. I'm sure you recognize that putting yourself through this ridiculousness is not the way to achieve that."

"That did occur to me and I felt myself almost back out, and I know this sounds really crazy, but I think they're really having the time of their lives now that they don't have to worry about me, that I've made it to that next phase of my life—getting married, settling down."

"Are you saying you're in love with him?" She's ignored everything I've just said because she believes I'm strong enough to get past all that. She's seen me get past much, much worse.

"Yes."

She screeches so loudly that I'm sure there is a trail of glass broken everywhere from Manhattan to the Pacific. "This is incredible. You know what's so funny about it? You are so in control of everything in your life and then you go and do the most incredibly impulsive thing you can do."

"Do you think this hasn't occurred to me?"

"Ha ha ha. It's just so ironic."

"Yes."

"Ooh, I'm loving this. I'm always the mess, but now, you, you're the mess. Even better, you're happy and it has nothing to do with all your planning and your ridiculous caution. I find this incredible. This is the best thing that ever could have happened to you."

"Although, oh boy," I hear her clicking around, "he has been with so many women. How do you even stand it?"

"Oh, I try not to think about it."

"I'm sorry. It's going to be hard. He's everywhere with women that are put on earth to make the rest of us feel average."

"That makes me feel a lot better. Thanks."

"But you know what? I bet it gets old having whatever you want, sex with whoever you want whenever you want. I mean, how could a person do that endlessly?"

We both break into hysterics. I know what it sounds like. How can any of this be real? It's so out of the realm of our experience. Is this, finally, why I'm fighting so hard not to push him away? "Hang on. I need you to *remove* that image from my mind, not burn it there forever."

"Yes, you're right. You know what would help you forget? Go onto the Louis Vuitton website and pick me out a luggage set. Tell your billionaire that this is the way to your best friend's heart."

"Thank you. Aren't you going to tell me everything will be fine, that Aiden doesn't need all those women now that he has me?"

"We all need to take risks in life. You, my friend, know that better than anyone. And besides, you didn't hire me to be your yes girl."

"I didn't hire you."

"Well, I took the job anyway. It's way too late now. I've already gotten this far. I wish I could give you a hug right now. Especially for the Louis Vuitton bonus you're getting me. I mean, it's so generous."

We both laugh.

"I wish I could hug you too," I say. I let out a huge sigh. "I haven't told you everything."

"You're pregnant!"

"No!"

"What is it, then?"

I hesitate. I don't want to paint him in a bad light in Jo's eyes when I've forgiven him, and yet I want her to know. I've taken such a leap. And I know it's the right thing, but I've been so wrong before. I take a deep breath and get it out. "There was a lie he told me. And that's made me a bit worried I've done the wrong thing trusting him." There, I said it. Progress.

"Ah, here we go, that's the Olivia I know."

"Thanks for your support."

"Again, not the reason I was hired. Tell Jo everything."

"He told me after we went through the whole fake relationship for the benefit of his father that there never was an ultimatum from his dad, that he just set that deal up so that we could spend time together because he knew he loved me from the moment he saw me."

"Oh yeah, that's a *huge* problem. No getting over that. How dare he fall head over heels for you? Give me his number, I'll give him a talking to. And seeing as how it turned out so badly, you being in some luxury hotel somewhere so exclusive people like me will never even know it exists, I'd say it's unforgiveable." Her droll tone exaggerates how ridiculous she thinks I'm being.

"I know. Rationally, I understand what you're saying. But the dishonesty does scare me. It feels like a sign I shouldn't ignore."

"Olivia, I know you wouldn't have gone down this road with him at all if this wasn't the real thing. For anyone—but especially for you—this is a huge leap of faith to have taken. Give yourself a minute to get used to everything."

"That's what *I* said!"

"See, Jo gets you. And I'm sure he'll understand if *he* gets you. But this is a man with a past. Can you accept that? Because I suspect that's a major reason you're doubting things, especially since you never let anyone in before. Picking a candidate like him, well, that's a major risk."

I think of his understanding words: *you're just as scared as everyone is of getting used to feeling this kind of love, this kind of care, intimacy, passion, this kind of feeling like you want to be under each other's skin, and then having it snatched away.* I conjure our kiss on my doorstep and my final summation: *fake?*

"He does get me. And he gave me a chance to say those things. And I almost chickened out. But he encouraged me, made it easy for me to find the courage to tell him that."

"Oh, Olivia, it sounds like he's doing everything right. And you're in love. You need to take the plunge. Now is your moment! I know you're scared. Sure, you could get sick again one day, but so could any of us. And he could do something that betrays your trust one day, just like Jeremy could do to me, *has* done if we're being honest—barring me from Google when I missed out on the fact that my best friend is engaged to a *billionaire!*

"Life is a full of risks—especially when we go after the things we really want. But if you're not going to go for the risks, what's the point? You'll be living a half-life, the way you have been for way too long, punctuated by reckless, stupid dares you take like following a dickwad like Corey."

"But what if the honest thing is just a game to a rich guy like Aiden who gets whatever he wants? Like he's seen this new place that I've introduced him to, and the challenge is attractive to him, but once he's achieved it, well, onto the next?"

"Well, that's the great thing about trusting yourself. You won't get into dumb situations like that. You learn to tell the difference, instead of acting out of fear and self-protection."

She's right. I've taken my trust—in myself and in Aiden—to new heights, but there's a distance to go. And I need to work on closing that up, even if it's scary. "Now *that's* what I hired you for."

"So, do I get my monogrammed Louis Vuitton now?"

"You've earned it."

"Okay, well since I'm on a roll, I'm reminded of something your mom said to me more than once. She thought your having cheated death all those times had to be because you were a very special person."

"Oh, God, don't make me cry now."

"It's true, and if Aiden Wheatley the billionaire has any sense, he's worked that out too. And that's why he's fallen in love with you."

"Oh please, this is not the movies."

"No, it's you. Who could make up someone like you?"

"All right. Fine. Thank you."

"You're welcome."

"I'm so happy for you, Olivia. I have a hunch that you're going to have a happy ending."

"You always say that."

"And I'm always right."

"Were you right with Corey? He was a loser."

"And, yes, I may have said that when things did look like they turned out badly, but that's because it always works out for everybody in the end. Though we don't know which direction will take us there.

"If we run into a Corey, drilling away at a redhead in our

bed, then we go a different way, and then things happen that we didn't expect, and that's where we find our true happiness. It's called discovery. It's called living outside our comfort zone."

"Okay, okay, okay, okay. Yes, every poetic bit of sage advice includes the words 'drilling away at a redhead.'"

"Well, what I'm saying is *this* is your happy ever after. That's what I'm putting my bet on. Twenty-five bucks."

"All right, that's wonderful. Thank you."

"You're welcome. Now go and tell your fiancé you're in love with him, that you forgive him, and you're ready to pull up your big girl pants and face your fears head on. Okay? Then bring me that fifty bucks. And my luggage."

"Will do."

"Great. I'll be following it all on Google."

"Thanks, Olivia!" I hear Jeremy call as she says goodbye.

THIRTY-TWO

OLIVIA

I really do have a lot of work to throw myself into, which is good because my home feels so strange and empty without him. I can't believe that in a few days' time, my life has changed so much. I bury myself in catching up on all the stuff I missed while spending time with Aiden tasting wine and making love.

There's a congratulatory email from the company news-letter on our engagement, and I can only imagine how badly that is going to be taken after the Poppy debacle at the Q&A. But gossip, I can handle. I've certainly had enough experience with that.

The next day I have a presentation to give Aiden, his father, and Charlie after lunch. It's about how to corner the market of women thirty to fifty-five, and it has all the data about where they spend their money, what they read, where they get their news, what their concerns are, what they're making salary-wise, what they want to be making, where they work, where they bank, where they invest, if they invest.

There are dozens of detailed questions about what they want that tell us exactly how to speak to them about the prod-ucts and services we offer. I know it's going to be good. The only hitch is I have a feeling that when I see Aiden, I'm going to swoon and forget what I'm talking about. Lord knows he won't make it easy with that smolder of his. And with everyone aware he's just become my fiancé, along with the Poppy incident, I know I'll have to be ten times better than the average data expert to be taken seriously.

I'm not going to let that get to me. I keep my head down, do everything that needs to be done in the morning.

At 11:30, I step outside the office for a quick walk and a healthy veggie sandwich for lunch and run into the wonderful Miss Poppy herself in the elevator on the way up. You can cut the tension with a knife. She is seething. I hope she doesn't say anything. If I get started with her, I don't know how I'll stop.

And past ten floors she doesn't. But finally, she turns to me and says, "You're not going to get away with it. Everyone knows what's going on here." I think I'm going to vomit. What does she mean? Does she know about the fake marriage? Surely not. I don't feel right. Did they know? Do they know? No way. Impossible.

I'm not being that woman anymore, driven by fear. Those days are behind me. "Oh, Poppy, you don't scare me. I've encountered so many Poppys in my life. Nothing you say is going to hurt me. You just make me stronger, happier to have made it through. So, thank you."

"Oh, don't thank me yet. You save that for later." The way she winks scares the crap out of me. But I'm not going to let that get to me. I've said my piece, I've made my decisions and I will stand by them. No more excuses.

Is it any wonder I'm off my game at the meeting? Thankfully I'm over-prepared, without thinking, I call off the numbers I've memorized from the slideshow. But I cut it short where I can, handing the men the printouts in report holders. This is not the presentation I needed to make. I'm so angry at myself for letting her get to me, but despite the fact that I'm not going to let the incident sway me, my mind is swirling.

The rest of the day is long and fruitless. I can't explain my behavior and yet can't correct it.

I start a fresh email and type Aiden's name into the recipient field. My fingers hover over the keys. I type, because I want to tell him about what happened with Poppy. I know this is the kind of openness that will strengthen us. He'd want to know. I want him to know. And that's a good thing. And I'm going to do it. But this is not the right way. It's too easy. It's a cop out.

I rise from my seat. I have to talk to him in person. There's no way we can go on like this. I turn and there he is, at the door to my office.

"Hey," I say. It's so good to see him.

"What was that before at the meeting? What's going on?"

"I just want to start out by saying that coming to you about this feels about as natural as—"

"A colonoscopy?"

I smile. He's good at this. And I know it's because he gets me. He comes in close, runs his hands down my arms. A current runs between us.

"What's going on?" He says it so patiently, so focused on me. It actually feels incredible to know how much he wants to comfort me.

"I'm sorry. I don't want anything bad to happen to you. I don't want you to disappoint your father... I don't know what I'm saying. I'm new to this. Let me start again."

His taut forearm muscles look stunning in his turned-up shirt sleeves as they stroke me encouragingly. I look in his eyes. I'm going to make myself say it, no matter the consequence; I have to be honest. "Poppy approached me in the elevator. She said she knew what was going on. I don't know what she meant. I told her she didn't scare me, but the truth is, her words have thrown me off. I know that you mean everything you've said. Your actions support that. I trust you. So please know it isn't that. But this trouble and resistance to us. It's . . . it's such a hard fight when it shouldn't be."

He pulls me in close, rubs the backs of my arms. "You know, Olivia, I've never had a woman I've loved dragged through this with me. I've had a lifetime of public slander, of everyone having an opinion to build up the strength to not give a shit. And look how that turned out. I was going to fake date someone to make myself look better."

I crack a smirk.

"I am such a lucky man in so many ways. But yes, there is an ugly side to this kind of money and exposure. Maybe this was too much too soon. Hey, I have an idea." He grazes his fingers all the way down to my ring finger. "Why don't we take this ring off?"

I do not expect the ice that freezes over my chest when he says that, slips it off and drops it into his pocket. "And just spend some time together. Out of the public eye, just you and me. Maybe that's what we need. No pressure. A trip. Let me show you the Australia you need to see. But first, let me take you to my place, and cook you dinner."

"You cook?"

"Yeah, I can cook. I didn't grow up in a barn. Is that a yes on the trip?"

"All right, what are you going to make us? And yes, that's a yes."

His smile flicks a circuit inside me. I love that I'm the one who put it there.

"I am going to make us some pasta. Real, beautiful, authentic pasta that I learned when I was spending a few months in Italy. It's quite delicious."

"Is it really okay to leave work for that long?"

"That's the benefit of being the workaholic boss who never takes a holiday. People are actually glad to see me go."

"And what about me? More fodder for rumors." I stop myself. "You know what? That's perfect. Give them something to talk about."

He jerks back. "Wow. You look so gorgeous when you say things like that."

"Is this your idea of dirty talk?"

He smirks.

We're building *our things*, the ones we'll circle back to again and again, the ties that bind us. And it is a moment I will never forget.

It's a bit earlier than closing time but he starts shutting down his computer, gathering what he needs. I do the same, and before I know it, Aiden's driver, Jack is driving us to Aiden's house. It's private, that's for sure, on the end of a cul-de-sac surrounded by uncleared land on either side.

The home itself surprises me. It's a two hundred-year-old convict-built terrace home with stone floors, original fireplaces, and towering cathedral ceilings. He takes me through every room, each more beautiful than the next. I count five bedrooms, one of which he uses as an office. Finally, we're at the terrace on the upper floor that gives the architectural style its name. Standing in front of the wrought-iron dining set out there, I can see the whole city.

Back in the kitchen, he pulls out ingredients and pours me a glass of wine. Soon enough, I feel more relaxed. I try not to play with the empty space on my ring finger.

At one point, I'm watching him toss the ribbons of pasta into the steaming, boiling pot. He looks so sexy in his white shirt rolled up at the sleeves. I just can't help myself. I move behind him, put my hands around him.

"What's this?" he says. He empties the contents of his

cutting board into the boiling water, which goes opaque, and then clears up. Strands of pasta bob to the surface.

"I want to be honest with you. Today, the reason I was off my game when Poppy approached me in the elevator, I was so affected by her words because it made me so deeply conscious of your past, all the women you've been with. It's my turn to step up, to bare my soul. I want to say that I trust you. Yes, your past, all the women you've been with, your reputation, they scare me. But I want you. And I'm not going to let that get in the way."

"Your honesty is the sexiest thing I've ever heard," he says. "But I'm not going to let Poppy get away with saying that to you." His jaw tightens.

I start to speak but he puts a finger at my lips. "Her behavior is inappropriate and she's going to be formally let go. Like I said, we don't tolerate bullying. And I certainly won't tolerate it toward you."

"What if she tries to fight it by painting you as someone who has messy entanglements with women he works with?"

"Let her. I'm up for the challenge. Nobody treats you that way. Now, we're not going to let her ruin another minute of our night. In fact, I'm thankful to Poppy for giving us this opportunity. The fact that you were so honest with me just now, showed me your fears. I know that wasn't easy. And it means everything to me. Thank you."

"You're very welcome. I feel so much closer to you already." And when he focuses the full force of his gaze on me, I feel pummeled by just how close we are.

"Well, that makes two of us. But this pasta takes just a couple of minutes, so that doesn't give me very long to show you how much closer I feel. Come here."

He lifts me onto the kitchen island, and I feel him stiffen between my legs.

Gently he traces his fingers around my forehead and down my cheeks. He kisses me so tenderly. It's explosive, like every truth we share adds the power of more dynamite to our connection. He pulls me to his strong, muscled chest. I feel warm and safe.

The kiss we share is my favorite so far.

When the pasta is ready, he dishes it up and we take it upstairs. There are a couple of candles on the table. Huge, old ones. "You spend a lot of time out here?" I ask him.

"It's my happy place. I mean, look at this view. I'm thankful for everything, and I also know that I'm in a position to make a difference in this world. And when I look out here and see how vibrant and hopeful everything looks, it makes me want to be a better man. And with the way you've shown your trust in me tonight, I believe I finally can be."

His words make my heart soar above the breathtaking skyline. I can only imagine the good he'll do if he just doubles down his determination, because he's already one of the most generous men on the planet. I've heard about his humanitarian projects. They are a big part of why I came to work for this company. It's no coincidence that my first growth hack for them has to do with equality for the sexes.

We dig into the heaps of pasta in our bowls, sprinkled with parmesan and parsley.

"Oh my God, this is delicious. Like the simple freshness has been given the perfect dish in which to shine, and so it knocks you out with its flavors." How does it feel like every word we say has a double meaning? *It's because your lives are becoming entwined; this is what it feels like to share with someone.* Within moments, we both devour our servings.

"Now, I'm going to ask you straight out, Aiden Wheatley, and I want you to know I'm saying this for all the right reasons.

And because I'm not afraid to trust you, or myself anymore—thanks to you. I want to marry—"

When I catch sight of what he reveals in his palm, I'm rendered speechless. The ring is in his hand again, as if he's had it there the whole time, just waiting for me to be ready.

"Do you want to wear this ring?"

I don't even have to think. "Yes, I want to marry you, Aiden —for real." And this time, it's not a question. I gaze into his eyes in a way that he can't misinterpret.

"It's always been for real, beautiful."

THIRTY-THREE

OLIVIA

The next few nights before we leave on the trip, we are a real couple. I stay at his house most nights and watch him make me dinner—turns out the pasta was his best dish, but he's honest about the bland chicken and the overdone lamb, so it works out fine and we wind up getting takeout more often than not. Plus, watching him do something imperfectly makes him so human.

And before I know it, we're on the road. And in a top-of-the-line white Tesla, and through the sky on the Wheatley jet, looping around my new home, three weeks fly by. I'm pretty sure I see everything Australia has to offer. Aiden makes sure of that. We start up north in Darwin, home of man-eating crocodiles, and some of the most treasured Aboriginal artifacts and locations on the planet. It's a whirlwind.

We stay at the best hotels. We sail yachts. We make love on the decks under the moonlight, drink the best champagne, eat the best lobster, dance to music from a band hired to play for only us. It's a dream. And if I know anything about dreams, it's that at some point you wake up. But it doesn't seem that way.

The next place we go is Queensland. We started at the far

north of the state in an area known for the rainforests where sugarcane grows and mangoes scent the air. Tree kangaroos jump from the boughs and platypus tip their heads up from the placid water if you wait patiently in a rowboat, which we do.

And we speak about the real histories of our lives, I've never been so honest with anyone, which clearly is ironic, and makes it all the more novel and sweet to expose my soul to this person, Aiden, who's captured my heart, body, and mind.

And when I share, he pulls me against his chest in the light of a fire pit on the beach, or in some decadent, 10,000 thread count Egypt cotton mountain of luxury we'd rented for the week. And he swears up and down that the world only existed to bring me to him.

Oh, part of me doesn't want to believe it, but hope has been flexing its muscles, getting better at this, and soon enough, I'm helpless as it floods every bit of my body. I swear that I'm done fighting it. *Make peace, not war,* I joke with myself, as if it was never a difficult thing to do in the first place. But Aiden's made it so easy for me to harness this strength.

I lose myself every time he looks at me with those sky-blue eyes, and kisses me, or turns me over on the bed, and makes love to me like we invented it. Like he can't wait to be inside and make me his again. And I can't wait for him to do it. There is nothing else.

We make our way down to the Sunshine Coast. We have no driver, it's just us. And I like it this way. With the top off the car, Aiden's hands on the wheel, his arm over my shoulders, exploring his playlist and mine, and the memories entwined with each, the endless road feels like it's ours, and I never want it to end.

We go to Byron Bay, and stay in a boho-chic villa full of stone and Batik fabrics, reclaimed teakwood, massive beds, and spare Aboriginal paintings that could say so much with only the dots of a paint brush.

We taste wine, and we taste each other. And if we weren't already in love, I'd say this was where it had happened, but we are, and that is clear. And so, this is just the binding.

"I love you," he says to me one night in Byron Bay. We aren't in bed. We aren't in the throes of passion. We are eating scrambled eggs. They are divine scrambled eggs, but they are just humble scrambled eggs, something I've had thousands of times before.

He puts his fork down with a chink against the plate. And he reaches for my hand. He looks into my eyes with those ocean blues of his and says, "I love you, Olivia."

"I love you, Aiden." It's the most natural thing to say it back. I can't believe there was a time when it wasn't.

And yet, later, while I'm packing our bags for our plane ride to the wine country of the Margaret River, after which we will fly home to Sydney, I'm surprised by a whisper of fear that creeps around me. This love is so big, it's no wonder I feel hesitant at going back to Sydney, to my parents' impending trip, where all our practice at ignoring the pressures of the world will be put to the test.

And then that old saying comes back to me: the bigger they are, the harder they fall. There is nothing bigger than this love. *But we won't let it fall,* I say, meaning every single word.

OLIVIA

Margaret River is my favorite stop on the trip so far. The place is spectacular—the scrubby grasslands and big skies shine like heaven—but I know the way its beauty resonates in my soul is enhanced by love, because I've let myself give in to it.

Aiden has certainly made it difficult to do anything otherwise, with his thoughtful tour, his never-ending series of surprises, and the honest way he enjoys making me happy.

I'd have to be a robot to withstand the torrent of love. The truth is I've never been happier. The days glow in joy and rich, fresh foods, and bold wines, picnics in the middle of nowhere, quaint, elegant homesteads on farmlands and vineyards. And the nights. Not that we wait until the night—the days have their share of illicit sex in the open field, his hands always seeming to find a way to make me crave him.

He gets a look in his eye like he has to show me I'm his, and there's nothing more my body wants, aching for him to take me, claim me, make me his again and again. I'll never tire of the look of his strong body over mine, his fists on either side of my head, driving into me, looking so deep inside me I know I'll never be whole without him again.

We ride that sweet rhythmic high toward climax, wanting it to last, helpless to give into the trance of orgasmic pleasure. Again and again, slick and wanting to feel my body hug his cock into that place where his eyes roll back and he screams my name, that delicious oblivion—Aiden and Olivia's pleasure, ours, ours alone.

It feels like a monolith of stone and steel, immovable during this time at a place of such beauty in all its forms. Margaret River is as diverse as the world itself—crystal blue ocean beaches, two million-year-old limestone, caves of gleaming crystal stalactites, forests of Karri trees and farm after farm of rolling hills, vineyards, and the namesake river itself, with its fields of velvet green on either side, the sun glinting on its surface.

This place, if I was poetically inclined, could be a metaphor for life's different faces, and in this light, it would be easy to believe that Aiden and I were strong enough to weather them all together. That ours is the rarest kind of love, strong as that ancient limestone.

On our last day, we decide to do nothing but enjoy the

beach. On the white, powdery sand, my head rests on Aiden's chest. I'm raw with the feel of him early this morning, thinking of the way he looked when lovingly soaping my body in the shower.

We fall asleep there. When we wake, we guzzle water like fiends and run hand in hand to the water, where we dash under waves, his strong arms never leaving my body, we float weightlessly over their crests.

Despite Aiden's endless entreaties to come in from the sun, I keep saying, "a little longer."

"I'm hopeless to deny you, but the Australian sun is not like in other places. It's incredibly strong. After this, we need to go in."

"Aye, aye, sir," I say, saluting him. Aiden pulls me to him and I'm lost in his kiss once again. Will I ever tire of his palms along my hips, exploring, teasing, loving?

We guzzle water as he instructs, and even something as simple as drinking the water he provides feels intimate and binding. I watch his mouth close over where my lips had been, take in the beauty of his bare chest, the bit of hair peeking out above his swim shorts. Then we walk along the shore as the sun sets.

As we gather our belongings at the blanket. I have to hold onto Aiden because a sudden dizziness overtakes me.

"Hey," he says, "drink more water." I watch as he unscrews the cap on the insulated bottle, but my head is throbbing. I feel lightheaded as I accept the water he tips into my mouth, his hands supporting my side.

"You are so hot. Shit. I knew we shouldn't have stayed out so long."

He mentions heatstroke, but this feels more like many of my darkest days that led to hospital stays, backward steps with friends and social events. The worry on his face cuts right to my heart. This look is exactly why I have never let myself fall this deeply for someone. How could I have let myself get comfortable here in his arms when I knew this was a possibility.

I keep mum. Besides, I feel myself breathing shallowly, my heart racing, and I couldn't string a cohesive sentence together if I wanted to.

I watch, knowing this is the end of things as we've enjoyed them these two months while the lifeguards respond to Aiden's calls, running over with a stretcher and bags of equipment. Everything is a blur as EMTs arrive minutes after, and they begin lifesaving procedure, oxygen and needles, manipulation and verbal direction, but one thing is constant—Aiden's eyes on me.

I feel them, and I want to meet them, but I can't. I know what kind of pain all of this brings, and I can't be the cause of such distress in such a magnificent man. I won't be.

"You will be okay," he says. "*We* will be okay," I think I hear, as if he can read my mind. But that must be me going out of consciousness, perhaps from something the EMTs have now administered.

I DON'T KNOW how much later I wake in a private hospital room. The first thing I see is Aiden. He's pacing the room, and my heart sinks. It all comes back to me. I am powerless to the tears rolling down my cheeks. I don't want to give him up, and yet I must. I will not be a drain on that regal man, will not dim his brilliant light.

I try to speak but my voice barely manages an inaudible croak.

It's been so long since I've seen the world from this perspective, and yet I slip back into it like an old coat, all the insecurities and fears, guilt and the sharp awareness of the burden that is me.

"Hey," he says, at my side, my face in his hands. He sits on the side of the bed, a knee splayed, looking like a work of art encased in worn denim.

"I'm so sorry," I say. My tears won't be constrained. The force of their deluge quivers my chin, twists my mouth. "So sorry, Aiden."

"What? What are you sorry about? It's my fault. I should never have let you stay out in the sun so long."

The sun? What is he talking about?

He can see the question tight at my brows.

"You had heatstroke."

"But only because I have a poor health history."

"No. The doctors said you are in excellent health. This has nothing to do with any of that. I see that look on your face. You are pulling away from me already. I will not allow it."

"You don't understand, Aiden. I know you think you're doing the right thing, that you can be here for me and everything will be okay, but I've seen how illness can drain the life from people you love and I know you want to be there for me. But it's so hard to know the pain I could cause you."

"Well, it's not your choice what I do. I will be the only person who makes that decision. Look at me, Olivia. There is nothing wrong with you. I told the doctors of your history. They rang your physicians in the States, who have also said you've been in excellent health for at least four years, mostly due to the excellent care you take of yourself. This is heatstroke—nothing more. You protected your skin with sunscreen, but you had too much time out in the intense sun that you're not used to. It can happen to anyone."

My head is shaking. "I know it's not true, but it's so difficult not to see this as a warning that I've been too complacent, let you in too far, relied on you too much."

"You're stronger than this. *We're* stronger than this. I love you, Olivia. And watching you open up and let go has been the most satisfying experience of my life. I will not let you go so easily. I can't."

"Aiden, I know it feels that way now, but when you wake up five years from now and your wife is in and out of hospitals, missing all the milestones in your life, preventing you from living the life you deserve, you will see things differently, and even if you can't, because you're blinded by your feelings, I wouldn't let you live a half-life that way. I will *not* be a drain on you."

"Not happening, gorgeous. I will not let you go. That's not going to happen to you, and if it did, I'd be there for you no matter what. Deep down you know that." His eyes are glassy and stern all at once.

"I'm sorry too, Aiden. I don't want to make this so hard."

"Then don't. You're letting me love you. You're giving me the biggest gift I've ever had. Just keep doing it."

I remember my promise at his house in Sydney, the night he put that ring on me for real. I nod, squeezing his hands tightly so he knows I mean it. Terrified as I am, I'm not going to run away because I'm scared. I'm going to trust my instinct, the way Jo had advised. I just may have to get her that luggage after all.

ON THE PLANE ride home to Sydney I'm tense. Just because you've dedicated yourself to doing something, doesn't mean it's easy. But I will not be swayed. We have everything. Nothing this luminescent will die. Not on my watch.

We've planned for me to go to my place alone, so I can sort out everything, get some belongings together to keep at his place. Outside my building, I say something incomprehensible about drawing a line under my old life, and he gathers me in his arms.

"This is just the beginning," he whispers in my ear.

He kisses me there, the feel of him on the sensitive skin is exquisite, making me want to pull him inside. But that terrible fear in his eye at the hospital won't leave me. I need this time, not just to organize my things, but my thoughts too.

"I understand. I do. But I wasn't scared. I just didn't want *you* to be afraid. I knew what you'd be thinking. We got this. You and me. We got this." Aiden tightens his arms around me, and in the strength of his embrace, I believe him. I tell him so, and the happiness this injects in his features is worth its weight in gold.

THIRTY-FOUR

L ike the doctors predicted, Olivia recuperated quickly. A few days' rest, excellent nutrition, and her vitals are all back to normal. But she looks like she's been through the wars. I wish she'd come to my place and rest, tell her that my place is her place, and this is where we should be when her parents come. But she insists she needs to go home and draw a line under her old life before she can start this new one with me.

And because she's put so much on the table, I believe her. "You do what you need to do. But I'll be missing you every second," I say. When we kiss goodbye, I lean in so she can feel how much I mean it. And boy, does my body show her.

At home, I take an hour on the treadmill and catch up on emails. Then my phone rings. It's Charlie. Not a name I want to see at 8:oo p.m.

"Poppy's not taking the firing easy."

"Well, we didn't expect she would."

"Says she's got the media all lined up."

"Tell her to go for it. I'm used to it."

"No, I don't think you understand. She's gonna sic them on

Olivia. *Aiden's paid-for whore* is the headline she's throwing around."

Just the sound of her name in conjunction with those words makes me want to punch something.

"Over my dead body."

"So how do you wanna handle this, boss?"

What I want to do is inflict a great deal of pain on her, but obviously, that's off the table. I need to handle this in person. I need to sit her down and tell her skanky ass how to behave like a proper human. And when that fails, I need to explain to her in no uncertain terms that she will not do anything to harm Olivia in the kind of language that she will understand.

I tell Charlie just as much and ask him to arrange for her to arrive here as soon as possible.

"Are you sure you don't want to wait until tomorrow morning? You know, clear heads and all that."

"Nup. I need to put a stop to this. Immediately."

"Okay. Expect her within the hour."

"Fuck, you are so stubborn, Olivia!" Jo yells into the phone. "Put the past behind you. You are not unwell, haven't been for years. And even if you were, is that a reason to mar your happiness? Do you know how rare the kind of love you've stumbled upon is?"

"Well, first of all, thank you once again for the show of support, love you too. But what I was going to say is that, despite the fear, I pushed through. I'm not home alone because I gave up on Aiden. I'm home because I need to wrap everything up here, say goodbye to all that negativity forever and get started—fresh—on my life with Aiden."

"Halle-fucking-lullah! I see my work here is done."

"I know there's a compliment buried somewhere in there."

"You bet your ass there is. I thought for sure you were going to fuck this up, honey. But you looked your greatest fear in the face and lived. If you weren't already taken, I might be falling a little in love with you myself."

"Well, who isn't?"

"I did have a little speech I prepared for you after our last conversation, when I was sure you were going to screw this up."

"Would you like to recite it?"

"You know me so well."

"Shoot."

"Well, you'd be saying all kinds of stupid crap about how you saw a look of fear in his eyes, and you have to put an end to it, blah blah blah, and I say, 'I put my loved ones through all kinds of other crap. Everyone does. Do you think there's a person in the world who comes without their share of issues, complications, and worries? Guess what the number one cause of death is in women around the world, Olivia! Guess!'"

"Heart disease."

"Give the girl a prize. Yes, heart disease! And what does that tell you?"

"That our global standards for female cardiac care are too low? Too much money given to military instead of humanitarian aid."

"Shit. I don't even know what he sees in you. You are so thick. You should give him my number."

"I'm sure Jeremy would be thrilled about that. And that was an excellent speech. I'm sure it would have done the trick."

"You're welcome."

AS POSITIVE AS my conversation is with Jo, as I start packing my belongings, sorting through the one box of Corey's pricey *jumpers* I missed in my eBay spree, with their hip sayings that I don't even understand, the more I realize the way to really show Aiden how committed I am is not here in this apartment.

That *drawing a line* bullshit was just a stall, because as far as I'd come, as much as I'd given, I was still holding off on that final step. A gesture like showing up at his house and staying there starting tonight, would prove to him how I really feel.

As soon as I think it, I start throwing clothes, my electronic devices, and my most sentimental items into a suitcase—a big one, one that says I'm here to stay. Had Jo's pep talk actually worked without her officially giving it? She'd love that, I think, smiling as I call an Uber to pick me up and whisk me to my new home.

AIDEN

Poppy. There have been so many women like Poppy in my life and it feels like a crushing kind of poetic justice that she's threatening the happiness I've finally found and fought so hard to secure with Olivia. Talk about your past coming back to haunt you.

But I'm not in it for the poetry. I'm going to protect Olivia, and I've done my homework on Miss Motherfucking Poppy. She's got some budget issues that she's been called on twice now. I could have fired her based on that alone. But the second I get off the phone with Charlie, I make some inquiries with the four companies for which the invoices don't seem to match up. Some pretty big bills for paper, toner, and office supplies.

The name Aiden Wheatley gets answers at 8:30 on a Thursday night because our business keeps these businesses alive. In fifteen minutes, I've got copies of invoices that don't align with the numbers she's submitted at all. I'm almost giddy with the idea of putting her in her place by her own misuse of power, when that's what she's accusing me of.

Jack, my driver, pulls up in front of my place exactly at nine. Poppy emerges from the back seat when he steps around to open the door for her. I'm amused to see that Jack's not above flipping her the bird behind her back as she walks away from the car. The guy's always been on my side.

She's wearing a raincoat that even I recognize as Burberry. I'm assuming I paid for that with the funds she skimmed from my company. Her slim, tall body is moving atop her razor-sharp stilettos in a way that's all about provocation, but not the kind Charlie was talking about on the phone.

Poppy is the kind of woman who trades on her sexuality, who viciously sees other women as opponents in this goal because they might stand in the way of what should be hers. Is she pretty? Yes, definitely. But the way she treats men like resources and women like obstacles is so downright disgusting that it renders her beauty powerless.

I open the door and immediately move back a foot when she leans in to kiss me on the cheek. She must be fucking kidding me.

"Oh, don't be like that, Aiden. There was a time when you preferred me to all the other ladies."

"No, there wasn't. There was a time when you were throwing yourself at me, when I was loaded and in a very bad place. And I'll own that. But it will certainly never happen again."

She flutters her lashes and splays a palm at her chest. "Ouch."

"This is a matter of honor. We're going to sort this out right here, right now."

I'm aware we're standing in the open doorway and I haven't invited her in.

"Aren't you going to ask if you can take my coat."

"No, I'm not."

Jack's taillights disappear down the other end of the spindly old street. I told him to give us twenty minutes. I'm thankful large swaths of trees surround either side of my place, and that we face in a direction that people can't see because I don't want a person in the world to think I'm associated with Poppy.

"Well, I might just take it off myself, then. It's getting hot in here."

"Suit yourself." I splay my arms, plant my legs wide, so she doesn't forget who's in charge here.

She takes a minute to untie her trench coat belt as if she's tantalizing me. I roll my eyes, making sure she clocks my reaction.

When she's got the ends loose, she works the buttons open and the lapels fall apart. She's got a slinky black lace negligee on underneath.

"Oh, for fuck's sake, Poppy. Don't make it worse. You're embarrassing yourself."

The street lights up. And she throws her head back, like I'm being amusing. A pair of headlights illuminate her. Then she lowers the coat off her shoulders and lets it slip to the ground. The car door opens and the world stops spinning. It's Olivia.

I run out to get her, but Poppy grabs onto me and puts her hand over my crotch. Olivia sees Poppy, makes a soul-witheringly disappointed look at me and gets back in the car. By the time I've pushed past Poppy and run to her, the driver is already around the cul-de-sac and racing toward the main street.

"Fuck!" I don't trust myself around Poppy, not with this anger so fierce I can feel it pulsing through my veins. I can't see straight from the force of it. Olivia will never believe me. This looks so terrible. And with my reputation, who can blame her for thinking the worst? Just when she trusted me enough to lean on me, to truly let me in to care for her for better or for worse.

I pull the mobile from my back pocket and try her number. She doesn't answer. I text.

AIDEN: Olivia, please answer. It is not what it looks like. Poppy is just being her manipulative self, trying to keep us apart.

Worse than anger and curse words, she comes back with nothing but radio silence. I ring again. No answer. At the sound of her voice message, I close my eyes, savoring the sound of her voice. "I love you, and I would never do anything to hurt you," I say. "I'm coming to tell you this in person."

I take a moment out in the street to breathe and get my anger in check. I can't go anywhere near Poppy without summoning some incredible inner strength.

She's got her coat around her now that the damage is done, but her smile, like the cat who stole the cream, is downright despicable.

"Look, I'm not even going to waste a precious minute with you when I should be talking to Olivia. You are the absolute worst kind of person. I've got all the evidence of your embezzlement."

"Embezzlement! Such big words! That's ridiculous!"

I pull the real invoices out of my back pocket and wave them in her face. "That's not what Sotag, Paperhouse, Donno's Office Supply, and Registered Inkworks think. And neither does the largest criminal attorney in the city."

"You wouldn't."

"Oh yes, I would, if you say one negative word about Olivia to anyone, ever again, I will press charges and make sure you go to jail."

"Or?"

"There is no *or*. I mean business, Poppy. Jail time. The max ten years—especially when I tell them about your long history of this kind of thing."

"Do you really think you're going to be happy with that woman?"

"I already am. And it's none of your business. And if you know what's good for you, you'll stay out of my business and the financial business in Australia for good. There's certainly not a person in the top one hundred firms that will hire you."

"Fine." She ties her coat up tight just as Jack pulls up in front of my lawn. I'm so glad he didn't witness any of that.

"You were a lot more fun when you were up for a party every night."

"It's funny you should say that, because it just goes to show you never knew me at all. I'd never been so miserable as I was on those nights, looking for something I would never find there—Olivia. Your little show isn't going to get in the way of that, so don't think you've walked away victorious in any way, Poppy. Time for you to go now. Your ride is here."

I turn around and close the door in her face.

But as enjoyable as that is, I've got much bigger things on my plate. Getting Olivia to forgive me.

THIRTY-SIX

OLIVIA

I'm so stupid! I cannot believe I trusted Aiden, only to find him an hour later with a naked woman on his step. And Poppy of all people! I must be the dumbest person on the planet to have believed him. As if someone like Aiden would ever settle down with one woman, an ordinary woman who isn't even near his league.

Just because I don't care about the money, the Gulfstream, the luxury hotels and service doesn't mean it isn't a thing. It is a very real thing. And it represents a rift between people like myself and people like Aiden that is too wide to bridge. I walked into a fantasy—a jaw-droppingly handsome billionaire who roped me into a silly little game that was probably just that to him.

As real as it felt, how could I have believed he was in love with me, that he wanted to marry me? And if he did, how could I have believed it was for the right reasons, reasons he so convincingly claimed were authentic and true?

I can't call Jo and tell her what happened. I just can't. Not after that last phone call where everything was so hopeful, when

I finally had the courage to jump whole-heartedly into this relationship with Aiden.

He rings. And texts. And texts and rings. He claims it isn't what it seems, that he loves me, that there is nothing going on with Poppy, that she was at his place to stop her from going to the media and ruining things for us.

But she didn't look like she was there to talk business. Unless that business was in his bedroom. The thought makes me physically ill. Besides, aren't those exactly the kinds of excuses men make when they are being unfaithful?

I think back to the earlier conversation I had with Jo, when she was Googling him, and every photo pictured him with a different woman. I should have seen it all along.

It's ironic, I think, as I lay in my bed and draw the cover over my head. We started with a lie, and now we've ended with one. I don't sleep. I stare at the ceiling, the pile of boxes I'd started to pack. The only thing worse than the pain I'm feeling right now, is the pain I'm going to inflict on my parents when they arrive in two days' time. Because at least I've learned one thing: my lying days are over.

THIRTY-SEVEN

AIDEN

After a sleepless night and one of the longest days imaginable, in which no action can seem to pass the time, I assure myself I have no intention of talking to Finn about my devastating situation with Olivia. In fact, I never talk to anyone about anything. What's the point? *Actions speak louder than words.* But I realize the gaping hole in my life her absence has created is about a whole mess of things. And talking about—wait for it—feelings (!) is one of them.

I can't talk to her because despite how clever, cool, loving, honest, or desperate my messages are, she's stonewalled me. If we ever get to the other side of this, I may need her on P.I.C.'s negotiations team. She certainly has the chops. But I know her silence is about disappointment in me, in having *trusted* me. And the worst thing about hurting her in that way is that, whether or not it was intentional, this Poppy blowup is a result of my shitty past actions.

I was so caught up in what Dad thought of me—and maybe even more caught up in pretending I didn't care what he thought—that I never teased out the root cause. And that seems insane from this vantage point because it's so bloody obvious that I've been behaving like a man who doesn't give a shit about anyone but himself.

Now, sure, I can go and put this on both my nature and my nurture. Like father, like son, right? But that's a fucking cop out and we all know it. What I need to do is own it. Not fucking blame it all on Poppy the way I have been. If I hadn't been the dickhead I'd been before I met Olivia, none of this would have happened. And if I want a proper future with her, no other explanation is going to cut it. I'm not that man anymore, because of her. And she needs to know that. I don't think a text message or voicemail is going to cut it.

I need to talk to her. But the action I'm gonna take to get there—it will be both grand and ballsy—is all designed to say the simplest thing: I need you just as much as you need me, maybe more. I need to learn from you how to drink the nectar of life, how to enjoy its sweetness in the way you do. And then I need to show you every day how thankful I am to have found you, and make sure you see and feel that love in every way imaginable.

Is the part of my plan where I create the opportunity to say these words a heck of a thing to do? Sure. But we had a deal, and I intend to keep up my end of the bargain.

In the meanwhile, I do find myself calling Finn. I walk out on my terrace as the call rings.

"To what do I owe this immense pleasure?" he asks by way of greeting.

"Can't I just want to say hello to my free-spirited self-made billionaire brother?"

"Sure. But I can't recall it happening before."

"Well, that's my mistake. You're right." I sit down and look out at that view. I can't help but layer Olivia's presence over even the simplest thing.

"This woman has changed you, brother. Never thought I'd

see the day when one was up for the challenge. And yet, here we are."

"Were," I say.

"Don't tell me you fucked it up already?"

"I don't think *fucked it up* even begins to describe the shit storm I've created." Unloading to him feels so strange, and yet I can also feel the connection, Finn's happiness that I've come to him. Needing people is such a strange but powerful thing.

I explain what went down with Poppy.

I can virtually see his head shaking, the smirk on his face. He's always said my behavior was going to bite me in the ass one day. Not in a talk like this, but in the kind of communiqué that involved forwarding horrendous news items—which, more often than not, included photos that required black-out strips over my dick—with bared teeth emojis. Despite that, he isn't the kind of guy to say, I told you so.

"You've got to get her back. If you don't, you'll regret it your whole life. She's a game-changer. I know you see it, or you wouldn't be calling me right now."

I tell him my plan.

Again, I know he's shaking his head, but this time I picture a smile spreading across his lips with that deep laugh. "If anyone can make it work, it's you," he says.

That's all I needed to hear. "Thank you," I say. "Really."

"You are welcome. Good to talk to you."

When I hang up, I look over the skyline as the sky prepares for sunset. The colors are soft and soothing, and Olivia would appreciate them. Perhaps she is right now.

I send another text message, but this time there are no excuses. Just honesty.

AIDEN: I'm looking at this incredible sky and thinking of you.

THIRTY-EIGHT

OLIVIA

The next day Mom and Dad's plane is due to arrive at 11:00 a.m. They'll have been flying twenty-four hours, all this way just to see their daughter is no longer engaged, and has retreated into the kind of mindset she left behind when she was seventeen. Oh, I wanted to throw that ring at Aiden when I saw what I saw, but I would not give Poppy the pleasure. Instead, I wrapped the ring box Aiden had lovingly given to me once we'd gotten home from our incredible day at the vineyards in a towel, which I slipped inside a cardboard box, and handed it to a courier to return to him. Without a note. I don't do mean very often, but I had a feeling that would hurt if anything he'd ever said to me was real.

And the more empty, pointless hours pass between that sight on Aiden's doorstep that I cannot seem to nudge into anything resembling sense, the more I am certain this wasn't Aiden being proven a liar. I do believe every word he said was true. But I think he bit off more than he could chew. In the end, for whatever reason—pressure, fear, habit—he slipped into his old ways. Even that, though, doesn't jive with the changes I've personally witnessed in him, the stunning ways he's opened up.

And that endless circuit of thought has been my entertainment these many empty hours leading to my parents' visit—because pondering the pain all of this will cause them is simply unthinkable. Better to just clean the apartment, confirm all the reservations, stock the fridge and triple check the itinerary spreadsheet.

They'll be so proud, I think, as I hold up the sign I made for them. *Welcome to Australia Mom and Dad!* I even drew three hearts, like a five-year old. I wouldn't do that for anyone else, but Mom is a person with a big presence. She likes grand gestures and I'm not going to rob her of one just because I'd rather blend into the woodwork.

I field my fair share of smiles and approving glances, and finally, they emerge from customs. I shake the sign and Mom literally runs toward me. Dad's trying to catch up, wheeling the luggage trolley, shaking his head in the loving way he's been trailing her for as long as I can remember.

Oh, and that hug. When I feel her arms around me, smell her familiar Elizabeth Arden Red Door perfume, my tears will not be held back. The reality of her love feels quite different than the worry I'd been contemplating these many months. *Jo's right.*

"My beautiful girl! Let me look at you!" She pulls back, her hands on either side of my head. "It's so good to see you. I've missed you like you cannot imagine."

"Judy, you promised!"

"I know, he's right." She shakes her head, her teeth gleaming in her huge smile, one that people have said is a mirror image of mine. "I can't believe we're actually here! Did you know on the plane, we had a girl with an Australian accent that was so beautiful. I was thinking, oh, you've got to get one of those, Olivia!"

"Mom." At least the tears are no longer threatening. She's so herself, all her idiosyncrasies such a comforting symphony that I barely know which way is up. Her bangs have grown to a normal length, and I'm so glad because I'm fighting so many emotions that one extra injustice for the mother I'm about to mortally disappoint would have thrown me over the edge.

"What? It's so cool. We're *Down Under*. I cannot wait to see a kangaroo. I was watching this special and I mean there are all the deadly snakes and all of that, too, but the kangaroos and the koalas and the wallabies. Oh my God, echidnas. Did you even know about these things? There's something called a bilby and they use it on Easter instead of a bunny. Isn't that crazy? I'm so excited. I want to see everything. I want to do *everything*."

"Mom, I missed you." She's just excited. Hopefully it'll wear off in a little bit.

Dad finally catches up and pulls me into one of his strong, wonderful hugs. Without a word, he shows me what I mean to him. I know the questions are about to come, my bare finger, the absence of my billionaire fiancé.

"Shouldn't have had all that Shiraz on the plane. Oh, but it was divine. Do you like that word? I got it from that stewardess. She kept saying, 'Divine, divine.' Oh, and you know what? We got bumped up to first class! Dad and I went to check in and we gave our names just like normal.

"I mean, I get a lot of points because I do all the supermarket loyalty over at Stop and Shop, but I mean, we didn't have *that many* points. Australia is totally on the other side of the world. And they said, 'Oh, Mr. and Mrs. Barker, you have been bumped up to first class.' And your dad was really skeptical. You know him. He's always such a bugaboo. He was like, 'Why?' And she said, 'It's just your lucky day.'"

Wait, just a minute. I have the craziest feeling that Aiden had something to do with that. It's got his name written all over it. I hear his words in my ear: *This isn't the end*. There's a fluttering in my chest when I think of the whisper of his breath on my ear. I officially hate my chest. No. He's the reason that I'm going to have to ruin all this happiness right now—him and his shock engagement. *In for a penny, in for a pound.*

"Family hug time!" Mom says. Sure, people are staring. A couple are sniggering. But we know what it means to Mom. We all get together and it feels amazing. I love my family. I don't care if my mom is wearing the world's most embarrassing T-shirt. I don't care if my dad bought the hat that I suspect is part of a costume in a bagged set from *Crocodile Dundee*. It just feels amazing to be with them.

"So, where's Aiden?" And here it is.

"Oh, well, Mom—"

She starts looking panicked. Oh God, I can't do this. I can't do it. I don't know what to do. I'm frozen to the spot. When all of a sudden, there he is. I blink twice to be sure my eyes aren't deceiving me, but he's still there. Looking and smelling *divine*. My heart skips a beat. Oh, that's happiness I feel at his presence, when all I want it to be is anger, which makes me determined to ramp up the anger to block that ludicrous happiness out.

"Hey, I finally got a park!" Aiden's waving and walking over to us like he's just a normal guy that drives a car and has to find a parking spot like everyone else. What the actual fuck? Like the reality of my parents' presence, the vision of Aiden in the flesh is something altogether different then the image of him in my mind that I have almost, if not quite, convinced myself I can live without. He's irresistible. And furthermore, he's sending signals that he won't accept anything less.

What is he playing at, shocking me this way? As if he did not understand me. No more games. No more reality. No more us.

"Oh my God, Aiden get in here. This calls for another family hug."

That smirk.

"Ah, I've never had a family hug. Let's see what you got."

Oh, I've never seen my dad look so happy. Can he actually like a man who is dating me? I mean, this is a person who has literally sat outside, oiling his shotgun the second I leave on a date, just so that the guy will know where he stands.

Dad's pat on Aiden's back, the grip he holds. I've never seen that before. And when Dad and Mom pull away, my dad's eyes are glassy and not in the way where he thinks his daughter's going to die. Oh, I guess I could just push the truth off a little bit longer. How can I not? They've only just arrived. And yet, it's just going to be so much worse now they've met him.

"Well, Judy and Rex. Is it all right if I call you that?"

"Of course. We're family." My mom puts her hand on his arm and looks at me with a double eyebrow bounce, like she approves. Maddeningly, this exchange is not lost on Aiden. I could only imagine how happy I would be right now if all of this were the genuine article, instead of a lead-up to a truth that's going to kill them.

"I thought you might want to stay at our place instead."

"Our place?" I say.

"Oh, did you not tell them yet?"

I open my mouth to say God knows what, but Aiden cuts me off. I give him the death stare. He smiles and ignores it.

"Oh, you know, we're getting married, Judy. It's not the fifties anymore. She's had her stuff at my place all the time and I just thought, well, why not just make it official? Right, honey?" He puts his arm around me.

I don't know what the fuck he's doing, but I just want scream. Mom looks wary. Dad's eye twitches slightly. And I think, oh good. Now they'll start hating him. That'll make it a bit easier to rip the Band Aid off and move on.

"Very sensible. Aiden," Dad says. "It's quite expensive here anyway, isn't it?"

Mom chimes in. "You guys will be saving money for the wedding. Maybe your little one's college education or as you guys call it—*uni*. Maybe you could tell me all about this whole gap year thing." And the two of them go off like two peas in a pod ahead of Dad, and I get the luggage. I cannot believe it. On the escalator, down to the baggage carousels, Aiden looks back and smiles.

There's something a little bit wicked about it, yes, but mainly he's actually beaming. Is it because he's won?

I'M SO ANGRY. I could strangle him. My brain keeps cycling through everything.

"Judy and Rex, we're right over here. We got a great park." So, he's decided to drive on his own. I guess he probably didn't want to be too showy in front of my parents. It's all I can think. Which is probably good because they would start feeling really uncomfortable, I think, knowing he had a chauffeur.

I mean, they heard that he was rich and famous, but they don't really do the Google thing. It was a neighbor who printed out the article and showed it to them. They still have America Online, I think, if that exists. Anyway, I can never get them to open an email and I certainly can never get them to look at any website links. They don't like that sort of thing.

"A *park*. Did you hear the way he said that Rex, instead of a spot? It makes so much more sense, doesn't it? I mean, a spot of *what?*"

But I wouldn't say he's exactly playing the humble card, because he has brought the Tesla, which is probably his most modest car, but still. And when they see the doors of the white space-age automobile rise, they both stop, goggle-eyed.

"Well, would you look at that." My dad says. "Like Batman." Why does everyone I know have to compare him to Batman?

I'm sure he will absolutely love that, and boy does that idea piss me off.

"Like Batman," Aiden says. "You hear that?"

My smirk can say a lot. But he's pretending not to hear it.

"Just like a married couple already," my mom says.

"Exactly. In fact, Olivia, give that hand here. I just got the ring back from the jeweler." He turns to Mom as he and dad heft luggage into the *boot*. "The stone was so big they needed to add some extra support."

Oh, for the love of God.

THIRTY-NINE

AIDEN

Sure, Olivia's pissed at me, but I can tell I'm already wearing her down. Like I was going to let her down on my end of the deal, make her go through this alone. Hell, I wouldn't do that even if I *wasn't* in love with her. But I am. And she is going to be my wife, so there's no way in the world I'm not going to show her parents how much she's loved.

She's scared to death. I get it. She has every reason to be. I'm a little bit scared myself—not for the reasons she was afraid of back at the hospital. I would give my life to have even a handful of moments with her—but because I don't even recognize myself anymore. She has so much control over me, it's not even funny. There's nothing I wouldn't do to be with her.

As for my surprise appearance, I don't know what's going to happen next, but I can tell it's going to be full of twists and turns.

When we get everyone to my home, I take Judy and Rex through the grand tour. They are impressed by the house, but they're so genuinely happy for us. There's no jealousy. There's no looking at me like I'm a different person. They're people, we're people.

It's a proper worldview I wish more people had. I show them to the room I saved for them. It's my favorite one. It's downstairs and it's got beautiful old opera doors that open to make a grand ballroom, but we have it closed off as a guest room now and it has this beautiful old Queen Anne bed larger than most people's rooms. It just looks amazing in there. I wish I could take credit, but my mom's the decorator and she's done an awesome job here.

They've got everything they need. It's as if she made the room just for them. It all feels so perfect—except for the look of death Olivia keeps flashing me.

"I'm glad you canceled that hotel. Didn't look half as good as this."

We all laugh.

"Why don't you guys take a little while to settle in and Olivia and I will start getting things ready for our first night together. I'm going to whip up my great grandmother's pavlova for dessert. It's the national specialty."

"Oh, Aiden, that sounds lovely." Judy puts her hands on mine and the look in her eyes is so genuine. "I'm so happy you're going to be part of our family. I'm bowled over."

"I am too," I say. I look at Olivia, expecting her to have the gleam in her eye that I do, but all I see is pure rage. I think I might've fucked it all over again. I am so shit at being the good guy, no wonder I gave it up so long ago. But difficult isn't going to stand in my way today. I can do this. In a flash, I see my error. Why didn't I see the risk that this move would feel to Olivia like me taking the control from her all over again? Because I'm new to all this. And this is the strangest motherfucking situation in history.

When I close them inside their room, I hear Judy whisper yell, "He said he's never had a family hug! Did you hear that? Poor guy. All this money can't buy happiness. Well, he's got us now. I'm gonna family hug the crap out of him." I smile. I can see where Olivia gets her warmth and spunk. I'm one lucky man, and even if I've gotten sloppy slotting in my second chance with the woman I love, I'm not going to let anything fuck this up.

"All right. I'm probably having a little bit too much fun with this," I admit. "I couldn't help myself from the first-class thing. I mean, what kind of self-respecting billionaire lets his future in-laws fly coach? That is not happening, so I did a little secret upgrade and made the woman at the check-in desk promise not to tell them who was behind it."

She knows they appreciated it. She thinks it's kind, but she doesn't want to say. She's not done being angry with me. But that's okay. I expected this. Things looked bad. And this was a ballsy move. Plus, she's fiery. And that's only one of the zillions of reasons I'm in love with her.

"Aiden, I can't believe you're here. I'm nowhere near done being angry with you. The only thing saving you right now is how happy my parents are. Which makes me exactly the dishonest person I said I'd never be again."

"Those are all fair points. I'm done making excuses. I will be very clear: there is nothing between Poppy and me. I would sooner gouge my own eye out than sleep with her. I love you and there is no one else. And I know it looks bad. It looks awful. And it *is* my fault that I've lived my life in such a way that something like this is even possible. And I'm sure it looks like Aiden going back to his old ways.

"But you have changed me. I am *not* that man anymore. Am I perfect? Hell no. But I'm working on it. You make me *want* to work on it. But before, I was so desperate for Dad's approval—and maybe even more caught up in pretending I didn't need it—that I never addressed *why* I acted that way. All of that looks so shameful from here. I barely recognize that version of myself. And I have you to thank for that."

She's softening to me. But I'm not going to rush her. We don't speak during the meal preparations, but when she fills her wine glass, she also fills mine. That's a good sign.

OVER DINNER ON THE VERANDAH, overlooking the city lights, Rex keeps talking about how he thinks the upgrade was because he mentioned his friend, Ricardo who used to work at the airport fifteen years ago. Her mom very sweetly, but very bluntly says, "That is the stupidest thing I have ever heard." He shrugs like he's heard it all before and yet he's going to believe it anyway. He doesn't wince from Judy's comment. Instead it's like two halves of a whole. She's right and he knows it, or he wants to know it, or will at some point. And that's why they work.

Their banter, back and forth, it's amazing. So different from the freeze-outs or knock-down drag-outs my parents hobbled into a marriage before they called it quits.

In the car, I went out of the way so they could get a glimpse of the sites—The Harbour Bridge, The Opera House, Fisherman's Wharf. It was a pleasure to see their unadulterated delight.

"Never in my life thought I'd get to see all this," Rex said. "That Ricardo," he said with a chuckle.

"Oh, Rex, look at the color of the sky here. It's such a different blue. What would you call that, Aiden?"

"Aqua? Reminds me of Olivia's eyes."

I look over and know she's dying to pull an eye roll, but everyone's cooing over how romantic I am, looking at her with such unadulterated happiness, she can't bring herself to do it. It takes everything I have to keep my smirk buttoned. This is not the time. "You know, Judy, when the painters came here from Europe, they struggled to represent the color because it was so different to what they were used to."

Rex had his hand clasped over Judy's the whole ride. They've been through it all, nearly losing their daughter again and again. And yet, here they were.

That's obviously going to take its toll on a marriage. My parents didn't have anything like that to struggle with and look at them, couldn't make it through five years without causing us all some serious psychological damage.

This is a family that works. This is a family that understands the things of value. And I want in. Still, Olivia's face when she saw me at the airport, priceless. I know I'm going to be telling that story on our wedding day. Even if she thinks this fake marriage or fake engagement is ridiculous, you got to admit it was a stroke of genius, because I certainly wouldn't be here right now with her parents otherwise, would I? She is special and I am never going to do anything that will cause me to lose her.

Did I get a bit hasty? Move a bit fast? Sure. But when you know, you know.

FORTY

AIDEN

"Aiden! How could you?" I can't believe how much her whisper-scream is like Judy's. If she wasn't so angry with me, I'd reach out and pull her in close to claim those lips with mine. I love her. I was never so sure of anything in my life.

"Olivia, you helped me, and I want to repay the favor." Why did I say that? First off, it's not the truth. Second off, I'm sure it's not what she wants to hear.

"I don't need any favors. That's how we got into this ridiculous predicament in the first place."

Amongst a whole host of choice words, Olivia has made it clear while she hacks at unsuspecting vegetables she's found in my crisper, that she has decided she's going to just tell her parents the truth about us and that my hijacking her plans is not going to change her mind.

"What they know will never get back to your dad, so you don't need to worry about that. Because we both know he will never trust you if he finds out this was all fake."

Ouch. But based on my past behavior, fair enough. Well played, angry Olivia. She only knows that because she knows me, because I let her in because she cared. And she still cares. I know she does. She's just scared and angry that I didn't honor her wishes. And I need to give her time to forgive me, lean on me. Her hands are waving like mad, so I gently grab hold of them, roll my thumbs over the inside of her palms.

"Let me start again. I did not come today to repay a favor. I came today because I love you. And I want to meet your parents like we planned. And I want them to get to know me and have a bit of fun planning some of the wedding with us while they're here. I know you're scared. I know you were trying to protect me and I think you know in your heart of hearts that I'm telling the truth about Poppy. And this feels like a bridge too far for all you've had to adjust to. But don't give up now. All I want is you —no matter the consequences. And I know you feel the same."

"What the—"

I haven't cut her off. She's gobsmacked.

"None of this was ever fake and you know it. You've always known it."

"I—" she still can't finish the sentence, but this time her shoulders deflate. I can see she's shifted her view, or at least decided to stop fighting it.

"And you also aren't jealous of Poppy or any of the other women in my past, because you know, in your heart, that none of them hold a candle to you. And even though it looks like that disgraceful scene at my place is just me being true to form, we both know, instinctively, where we stand with each other, and that I am not that way anymore. We've known since that first minute. There was a spark.

"It woke me from this dead, cold sleep I've been in my whole life. And it woke you from playing it safe. But now that it's real, you're scared. You're terrified because you think one day you might be sick. You mind is saying, 'What if I have to lean on Aiden the way I did my mother? What if he spends his life worried sick over me? Or worse, what if I die?' And what happened at my place gives you an easy out so you don't have to worry about that anymore. Well..."

I look into her eyes and pull her close. "The only thing I would ever regret if that happened was not having this time with you. I'm not going to let any of those worries get in my way. Now please, I beg you not to, either. It is my greatest honor that you care about me so much that you would sacrifice your own happiness for mine. But that is a mistake, Olivia, I can't be happy without you. Surely you see that. Please tell me you'll marry me—for real."

"How do you know me so well?" There are huge, heavy tears streaming down her face.

"Because you're my other half. I saw you across the room of that hotel and noticed it right away. You're the reason that girl threw her drink at me. I couldn't keep my eyes off you."

"Well, who could blame you."

"Is that a yes?"

"Of course, it's a yes."

At that exact moment we both notice Judy and Rex standing at the doorway.

"How much did you hear?" Olivia asks.

"Everything."

I can see the color drain from her face.

"Listen, we're not even going to ask!" Judy says. "When you find true love, it makes you do all kinds of crazy crap. Let's get that pavlova you promised us and brew some coffees so we can get back up here and tell you all about how your father kidnapped me when we were twenty, and your granddad nearly shot his ear off! But that was only after your dad finished trying to make me jealous for a couple of years with my former best friend."

Aiden and I look at each other. I'm not sure I want to hear that.

"I cannot wait to get into that one." I slip my arm around Olivia and pull her close. "But first I want to let you know I will never do anything to hurt your daughter. My sole mission in life is to make her as happy as she makes me, just by being her."

"I've felt like that since the moment she was born," Judy says.

Are those tears in my eyes? This family is going to kill me, in the absolute most wonderful way ever.

"Family hug?" I say, not even trying to cover the tears. "In for a penny, in for a pound."

AFTER DINNER, our bellies are full from my famous steak and sausages, the charring of which, I apparently inherited from my father. Olivia's parents have politely chewed through making all the right sounds, but Olivia takes one particularly long moment of silent gnawing on the filet steaks to say, "Aiden's dad burns his steaks, too."

Judy scolds her daughter for being rude, but I come to Olivia's defense. "She's right. That's why we're good together. We're not separate people anymore. I suspect you know what I mean, Rex," I say. Olivia's dad lets out a huge exhale. "Yup." We all laugh at my staggeringly poignant observation of the reality of love. I barely recognize myself. And judging from the beaming Olivia is doing as she slips my arm around her shoulder, that is a wonderful thing.

Judy sets down her cutlery and clears her throat.

"There's something I can't seem to get off my mind," she says, looking between the two of us.

Here it is, the moment she's put together the dregs of our conversation. When she can no longer stand gnawing on the husk of whatever *the truth* might be, when she must know what it is.

Well, I can't let Olivia tell them—not after all I've put her through, not after what she's done for me, and mostly because I love her and this hurt she's been trying to avoid is absolutely pointless.

"What exactly was it you were going to confess to us?"

She parts her lips to speak, but the words come shooting out of my mouth. It feels like covering her with my body in a shower of bullets.

"We're pregnant!"

Mom and Dad are so excited they don't even notice the daggers she shoots my way.

FORTY-ONE

OLIVIA

My parents close the door to their room after dinner and Aiden and I are finally alone.

"Pregnant?" My head shakes and my hands are planted firmly on my hips. But I forgive him. For that and for everything.

I'm helpless not to.

I love him, and everything is so right. Am I scared? No, I'm terrified.

But he looks at me with those ocean blue eyes and he calls me on it. "You're terrified. I know that. But we're in this together now. And that is what makes me who I am. From the moment you walked into my life, that's the way it's been. And there's no going back. My happiness depends on one thing and one thing only: you let me in, you share your life—good and bad —with me."

It's pointless to resist. We can spend our lives punctuated by moments like this, while every other one is spent protecting ourselves from the possibility of hurt that may or may not come our way. Or we can live.

"Okay, you win," I say.

"I always win," he says.

And for once, I'm glad that's true.

When he takes me in his arms, happiness, comfort, safety and love wash over us. It's so right. He grazes my arms with his fingers and that heat is instantly between us, but it's layered in security, trust, and a fierce loyalty that is emanating from his touch as much as it is glowing within my chest.

Aiden lifts my face to his and our lips and tongues urgently struggle to express all that we feel. We're going to have a hell of a night.

As he takes my hand and leads me to his bedroom, I say, "I guess we don't have to use protection if we're pregnant already."

"I have never heard you say something so sexy."

I stop halfway up the stairs. "Under one condition."

"What's that?" he says, one eyebrow arched.

"You let me teach you how to cook a steak."

I can see his ego dart up, but he's a man of action. He said that a long time ago. And now he's called me his other half, so what will he do?

"Of course, right after I show you a thing or two up there." He thumbs at the bedroom we're headed to.

"Now that's a proposal I cannot pass up."

He presses his body to mine, and effortlessly picks me up, my legs curling around him, and carries me to bed.

EPILOGUE

OLIVIA

O ur wedding will be small. And that's no thanks to Aiden, who wanted to invite everyone under the sun to our wedding. "I want to show the world how much I love you," he says.

But after all the things we did for the benefit of other people, all I really want were the people who matter, the ones I genuinely want to share our love with. And in the end, he comes around to the idea.

We couldn't decide between having it at the Grand Hotel or the Cockfighter's Ghost vineyard, because both places were special to us. But in the end, we decided on the Grand Hotel—it was where we first experienced our insta-love, even if it took quite a while for us to admit to.

"Besides, if we go the other route, people are going to be cracking cock jokes for the rest of our lives," I say.

"God, I'm so glad you said that," Aiden says, "because it sounded so childish, I did not want to be the one to say it. But it is so true. And you're so sexy when you say *cock*, even when you're joking." I elbow him, we laugh, and yeah, it's childish, until he grabs me by the arms and whispers into my ear, "Say it again."

And maybe that juvenile joke shouldn't be the sexiest moment of our relationship. But it is one of many that compete for that title during the months leading to our wedding.

And I know that all these are the moments building the foundation for our future—the childish jokes, the mornings without makeup, the way Aiden looks when his eyes flutter open in the morning, the way he likes a hamburger.

That night when we book our wedding at the venue that will go down in history as the *cock place*, we order in pizza and show each other our favorite movies. We wind up talking until the sun comes up after we finish the second film. I will never forget a moment of that night. And that's because it turns out to be very special for a reason we'll treasure for the rest of our lives ... more on that later.

OLIVIA

The wedding is a dream come true. It is literally the happiest day of my life. Mom and Dad and Jo are here, my mother's sister and my only living grandparent, my dad's mom, all of whom we flew here on our private jet.

Aiden has insisted they all stay with us. He has never experienced this kind of family bonding before and it is incredible to watch him drop the self-contained demeanor and laugh and touch and lean in to people who care for him in a way that has no strings and no guilt and no clauses.

It's made him understand how to communicate with his own mum better too. After years of protecting her and treating her like a fragile thing, he can finally be himself, and she's told me it's a joy to see him this way.

"It's like going back twenty years. He used to be such a bright-eyed, open boy. And it has killed me over the years to see that my staying with his father for the peace and security I thought the boys would benefit from only made him feel like he had to put on a front for me." The way her husband rubs her back to support her through this conversation speaks volumes.

When her tears fall on the night of the rehearsal dinner, it's just the four of us enjoying a quiet drink before we head to the restaurant. I explain to Eleanor that I did the same thing with my own parents, and that her son is the reason I was able to open up and start living for myself.

It's at this moment that Eleanor and I really start our special relationship. I think it's because she sees that I understand what is special about her son. And that I appreciate him for reasons no one else could.

"I'd say welcome to the family," she said. "But I feel like it's you welcoming me in."

"She has that effect on everyone, Mum. You're going to have to get used to it."

"Well, it will be my pleasure. Milly can be a bit of a handful."

"Oh, she loves you so much, Mum!"

"I know, but does she have to say it quite so much?"

"Yes. Yes, she does."

"Ah, I know. And we love her for it. Both of my sons have made our family such a special group."

AIDEN

Since the whole world is staying at our house, we rent a hotel suite for our wedding night. And shit, is it a good one. It's the penthouse at the best hotel in town and it's got 365-degree views of Sydney. The harbor is sparkling in the moonlight and the skyscrapers are glinting and lit up and it feels, from this perspective, like it's all for us, which is exactly what I wanted for my beautiful wife.

She's still in her dress looking even more perfect than I could have imagined. Her neckline dips low, *tastefully* she says, and it's certainly to my taste, especially when she leans over and what she calls *the delicate drape of it* drapes off center and gives me an eyeful of those breasts that drive me wild. Is it wishful thinking, or is her middle looking like those lies I told when Olivia's parents first came to visit have come true? I can only hope.

I slip my hand over her bare shoulders, run my fingers down to her wrist and up again, then take her delicate bare back in my palm, letting my hand explore beneath the silk to grab onto that full tit that I am going to take into my mouth for the first time as her husband.

Just the thought of it makes my cock throb. I squeeze, my hand expressing to my wife the intensity of my need for her tonight. Watching your brand-new wife, who has opened the world to you in a way you never knew possible, glow in the happiness of making it official with you while everyone in the room reflects the brightness of her love, when all you want to do is bend her over the bar and feed her every centimeter of you, while her wet, hot, pussy hugs you in that way that makes you drive into her like a man possessed—well, that is a kind of sweet torture that brings you to the frenzied, lustful desire I'm one hundred percent full of at this moment.

We're on the balcony, taking all of this in and she's squirming to let my hand in farther. And that's all I need. My other hand is bunching the skirt of her dress up madly, loving the feel of unwrapping her, but needing to get to the sweet honey of her cunt.

When I've got access, I see her sweet round ass in the naughty little lacy panties she wore just for me. There's barely anything to them, but what's there is teasing, revealing, and the kind of dominatrix style I've never seen her in before—with straps I snap onto her taut cheeks. She jerks and her breath catches at the feel of the band on her skin.

"Now this doesn't seem like the kind of thing a good wife wears on her wedding night."

"Well, I'm not sure Aiden Wheatley would marry a good wife. He would want a naughty one. The kind who would pick her dress up—" Here she takes the meters of silk from my hands and lifts them out of the way, hefting herself onto the table, spreading her legs, pulling the whisp of lace away to reveal those sweet lips.

Now it's my turn to stop breathing.

"—And spread her legs, and tell her husband to fuck her,

while she teases him a bit by slipping her fingers around on her wet clit for him to watch."

I am mesmerized while she does as she promises, her eyes on me the whole time, her body reacting to the pleasure of her finger dancing around her folds, circling her nub.

I unbutton my shirt, love the way she shudders at seeing my chest, her tongue darting out and licking her lips like she wants a taste. I unbuckle my pants, slowly lower the zip as her eyes catch every second, and let my cock bob up in those gray briefs she gets instantly wet for.

I get on my knees and pull her by the ankles so she's at the edge of the table. I push those thighs as far apart as they'll go and lick her rich honey from her fingers. She's trembling, so close already.

I go in, use the flat of my tongue to lick every bit of her, from her opening to her rosebud clit, then I softly lick deep into her folds. Back down to her molten core, I thrust and thrust my tongue deep inside her cunt, losing myself in an overload of having her, tasting her, feeling her, hearing her moans of pleasure.

Then I replace my tongue with one finger, watch as her eyes fall back and her lashes flutter like an addict getting her fix, then I thrust a second finger inside of her and enjoy the way her hips rise and buck into me. I lean back in and tongue her nub like mad as she fucks my face and fingers, her body and juices over me are pure bliss. In an instant, she's gone stiff, her hips as high as they'll go, and she's twitching and yelling out and coming all over me.

I need to be inside of her. We've tried to be good and use protection when we had sex—and succeeded every night except for the movie night, when we fucked ourselves into a whole new phase of knowledge of each other's bodies. But tonight, I'm going bare by intention, taking my wife in the way man is meant to.

I slip those panties all the way off and have a good look at her cunt, still quaking from her orgasm. I lower my briefs, the only thing separating us now, and enjoy the look on her face as she sees my cock bob free. I let it press against her, feeling the thrum of the pleasure I've just given her as I take her face in my hands and kiss her, letting her taste her juices all over my mouth, the way I like it.

My naughty little wifey goes limp with pleasure then goes in harder, sucking my tongue and raising her hips like she wants my cock right this moment.

Oh, but not yet, baby.

I lower my mouth to her tits, licking, lapping, biting as my cock teases at her opening. She's squirming, moving my crown so that it's so close to her opening. Now I gasp. We're right there, but we don't move. How long can we wait in this delicious torture?

Her hands make their way to my shaft, pulling as she works my tip at her cunt. I jut suddenly and she arches, yells out.

"No," she says. "Not yet." But her body hasn't gotten the memo because she feeds me inside her, easing all the way down to the hilt.

"Okay," I say, and slide myself out torturously slow, while her eyes roll back in ecstasy.

I tease around her sweet honey, enjoying the sensitive, heightened tingle of every place our bodies make contact. My brain overloads on the echoes of electric reaction.

"I can't take it anymore. Fuck me," she says.

Hearing the words from her mouth, I growl, turn her over so her sweet ass is bare before me. I pull her up high, tilt her hips, then work my tongue up and down her seam. She jiggles desperately before me.

"Fuck me," she says.

I brace my hands on her hips and slide inside as my body is all pulsing—my heart, my cock, my need, it's wrapped up in a bundle of lust so tight, I am nothing but the driver for it to spring.

I watch as I thrust into her again and again, her walls hugging me in a way that I just can't get enough of. But each time I slide inside her beautiful wet pussy, it brings me closer and closer. I don't want it to stop.

"God, I love you, Olivia."

I lean farther over her, pull her back to meet me. I catch sight of us in the mirror across from the bed. It's perfection. I run my hands over her tits, pull tightly on her nipple, and she rocks so beautifully, meeting each of my strokes. I reach down, my hand feeling at that wet nub, and she yells out, which makes me thrust harder. Her eyes squeeze shut and she shudders around me.

"Come inside me," she says, staring me down in the mirror.

I'm a man lost. I feel the overload of my body, a tingling springing free from the backs of my knees, the hairs on my neck stand on end, and I come inside her in a wave of orgasm I'll never tire of.

AIDEN

Have you been to Bali? Nicest place on the planet. Rich culture, warm people, and boy, oh boy, do they know how to do luxury. This is why I take my sexy, beautiful, incredible wife there for our honeymoon.

I want nothing but expansive experiences for us. She gave this world and all its riches to me—a stupidly rich man who wasn't even enjoying life's best bits—and I want to give it to her. It's how we work. She's the yin to my yang. And so I want to yang her yin as a wedding gift.

We climb ancient steps to the top of Buddhist temples at sunrise, we watch dancers in painstakingly batiked costumes with headpieces of bronze, and leonine eyeliner, hypnotize us with their elegant, synchronized, ancient movements. We ride a moped in the crazy streets, two of a billion people weaving this way and that in a frantic evening commute, to stop at a restaurant where the plates of food are works of art and the people who bring then are as warm and welcoming as my beautiful wife is to everyone she meets.

She buys too much batik. She loves the wooden puppets

and the carved teak furnishings for our home. She makes friends with everyone she meets. We love our month here so much, we never want to leave. And I'm so rich I say, fuck it. Let's stay another month. And we do it. Until that month is cut short.

It's the end of another full day of beautiful beaches, incredible culture, indulgent food for the senses to feast upon, and I'm waiting for my wife to emerge from the bathroom. We've just had a long soak in our incredible tub and the kind of sex that one doesn't picture when they think of blushing brides.

And instead of our customary inability to stop staring into each other's eyes afterward, our hands not quite able to let go of each other's skin, she drains the tub and shoos me out.

"What are you up to?"

"I have a hunch. And I'm about to confirm it."

I'm a smart man and I work out this riddle instantly. I leave the bathroom without a fight and sit on the bed, a plush white towel around my waist. I find my hand is trembling. Am I about to find out I'm going to be a father?

If I thought my love for Olivia couldn't get any stronger, I certainly hadn't contemplated this moment. It feels like an eternity before she emerges from that room. And I can tell by the smile on her face that the news is exactly what I want to hear.

I shoot up from the bed and lift her off the floor and into my arms. I wait for her to say it, though the smile in her eyes and on her lips says it all.

"You're going to be the best father," she says.

I smile so big, I can feel it stretch my face. "Only because I have the best wife. Thank you. Thank you for walking into my life, thank you for falling into my trap. And thank you for making me the happiest man in the world."

I claim her lips in that way she says will always make her knees buckle, and I feel loved and powerful and like everything in the world I could ever want is mine—to care for Olivia and bring her happiness each and every day. I hold her in my arms in the way that told her I loved her before we could bring words to articulate it.

"I do have one question, though," I say. "Is this how our whole marriage is going to be? We say something's true and then it happens? Because I have a few ideas right now I'd like to give a try."

Olivia flashes that ten thousand-megawatt smile and goes to bat me, but I grab her hand in time.

"I'm just kidding, gorgeous. I already have everything I could ever want." My mind flashes back to the night when we ordered in pizza and binge-watched our favorite movies. The doctor confirms the date of conception in a few weeks' time, but I don't need the scientific proof to know that most intimate night was the evening our baby was conceived.

"And don't you forget it, Wet Shirt."

She places my palm on her belly and pulls me in for a tight hug.

"Family hug," she whispers into my ear. "*Your* family hug."

THE END

While you're waiting for the next SUCH A BAD IDEA book, scroll down to start reading KEEP CALM AND PERFECT YOUR SMOLDER right now!

Keep Calm and Perfect Your Smolder
The Flame Series
by Daniella Brodsky

CHAPTER ONE
MAGGIE

"SO WHO ARE these people we're eating dinner with again?" Reg looked at her as if this was brand new information he was inquiring after.

She'd told him twice but he'd been fiddling with his phone while the taxi waited at an endless red light, and she knew he hadn't been listening. She wasn't sure he was listening now, even though he was looking right at her. Later, he'd probably say she'd never told him their names. There was no point in arguing. He was hopeless at remembering details like names, birthdays, appointments.

That's why they were running late now. He'd been at the gym and she'd been pacing the apartment, trying his mobile to no result. When Reg sauntered in with a podcast turned up so loud her eye began to twitch, he stopped before he'd closed the door to answer a text and hadn't even noticed her standing in front of him with crossed arms.

He jumped when he saw her, and in the process dropped the phone he was using for yet another text message.

"Maggie! Why are you sneaking up on me like that?"

"Reg. I've been ringing you for an hour. We have that dinner with Florence from my work tonight. I put it in our Google calendar and on the calendar on the fridge. We spoke about it on the phone this morning."

"God! I hate calendars! Why do we have to go out on a Friday? It's been such a long week. And you didn't—oh, there, twelve missed calls? A bit much, no? What are they, Kennedys?" He sat on the woven bench and yanked at his shoelaces while she tried not to think how his sweat was going to stain the rattan.

"Please just get ready Reg. I've texted them to let them know we're going to be late, but we were meant to be there in ten minutes. It'll take us at least triple that to get to the harbor."

"If we live in Paddington, where the best restaurants in the city are, then why are we going all the way to the end of the city?" He pulled his shirt over his head and let it fall on the bench beside him. He put the stinky trainers on top of it and left it like that. The running was slimming him down too much. Reg was naturally fit and now he was losing whatever bulk his chest had. And she'd really liked that bulk.

"I will tell you again in the taxi, but for now, please go shower." Thankfully he made his way down the hall. In front of the laundry room, he stepped out of his pants and kicked them close to but not *in* the hamper.

Maggie bent down to pick them up and recoiled at the soaked nylon.

"I don't know what to do with myself," he started to sing as he fiddled with the shower mixer and steam billowed into the hallway to destroy the sleek hairstyle she'd brushed, ironed, and smoothed into obedience earlier.

They were going to the Darlinghurst eatery because of the tasting menu. She and Florence were in the food biz. They were on the planning side these days, rather than behind the fry pans, but they both endlessly went on about getting back to their cooking roots. Neither of them had discussed practicalities, and usually there was wine involved in their oaths to do so, but Monday morning saw them both at their desks, planning and researching, rather than in the trenches.

She wasn't unhappy at Five Dinners, Done!, the meal delivery company taking over Australia, but she wasn't exactly happy either. Except when she spent time with Florence. They'd been promising to do this dinner thing for at least two years. And now here they were. Rushing, stressing (at least *she* was), but Maggie promised herself she'd calm down in the taxi so she could have a good time with her friend.

It would be great to take their friendship to the next level. And Florence's boyfriend, Lionel, was meant to be fun and exciting, according to Florence anyway. Maggie couldn't help thinking his name promised the opposite. *Lionel? What kind of name was that?* Something from a children's book about a wiley lion, it stuck in her craw.

He was in the military, so at least they'd have something to talk about. Maggie had grown up in a military family, and had worked on Fort Bliss for five years before she'd emigrated to Australia because of he who would remain nameless. But that was a long time ago, and surely she could go over those times without showing any signs of distress.

REG USED a card to pay the cab fare and it took forever. The driver had to reboot his payment system twice. She itched to use the emergency fifty she kept in her purse, but she knew that would piss Reg off now. He never carried cash and sorely resented it when she was prepared and he wasn't.

Fine. She'd walk in ahead.

The restaurant was in touristville, right at Sydney Harbour, with floor to ceiling windows overlooking the bridge, the quay, and the Opera House. As she climbed the stairs two at a time, she peered out the pristine glass to appreciate the view. It never got old. Sometimes she rode a ferry just for the purpose of appreciating it. It was like a little visual reassurance: *yes, you got it right coming here.*

Reg would catch up. The glamorous woman at the hostess stand asked for her name. "Maggie Jones," she said. "Table for four. We should have two people here already."

"Yes. You're very lucky. We're not really permitted to seat parties until all the guests have arrived, but *Lionel* was so persuasive, I let them." She shrugged, like, *who could resist him?*

Maggie hated him already. Which was unfortunate, as she'd pictured the four of them renting adjoining cabins on the South Coast and grilling steaks and snorkers over a campfire—even if Lionel's face was out of focus in the images.

"Let me take you." The woman's cascading blonde waves were picture-perfect. They swayed as she led Maggie.

She looked back, but there was no sign of Reg. Good. Let him sit there for an hour watching the taxi driver reboot the credit card device. If he needed her, he'd ring, surely.

How many nights had she spent listening to his friends drone on about financial jargon she couldn't even decipher? The one night she proposed to do something with *her* friend and he had to go out of his way to ruin it. She wouldn't let him. She happened to believe we were each the master of our own fate.

Still, she tried his phone as she followed the hostess's mesmerising hairdo around the winding dining room. He didn't answer.

"Maggie!" It was Florence, and she got the same punch-in-the-gut gratefulness she always did at the sight of her. Florence was waving her down frantically, as if she had been afraid Maggie would never actually show up. She wouldn't sell Reg out, but she wanted to.

Her friend ran over to her and her dense corkscrew curls, which she'd let hang loose this evening, blocked the view of the table she'd come from.

"I'm so glad you're here! They've given us the most amazing amuse-bouche while we were waiting! We'll have to get them to bring you one. I cannot wait for you to meet Lionel. Oh, look at me, going on like a teenager! Too much bubbly already I'm afraid. But oh well, you'll just have to catch up." Florence firmly gripped Maggie's arms and smiled like she couldn't help it. There's was a natural kinship and there was no resisting it. Maggie felt sure her own smile was just as revealing.

Maggie hugged her friend firmly, thankfully, and nearly felt a tear spring to her eye. God she loved this girl. Sure, she'd had close friends before, but these two had a chemistry, as if they'd always been friends, but had needed to search the world over to reunite. It was effortless and rewarding—a rare combination.

"Come, come," Florence said, and pulled her to the table that sat the man Florence had told her so many intimacies about she could probably write a whole book about him.

The hostess moved away from a private joke she was leant over the table to share with the famed Lionel and that's when Maggie saw him. No. It couldn't be. He looked an awful lot like George.

Mother of God, please don't let it be him. She stumbled for a second on her heel and bent over, as if to straighten it on her foot, but what she was trying to do was blink the image away, so when she stood again there would be Lionel, Florence's boyfriend at the table, and not George, with whom she'd fallen madly in love all those years ago in Fort Bliss, accepted a spur-of-the-moment invitation from to emigrate to Australia, only to then suffer through the worst break-up in history. As far away from home as a person could be.

She'd been "seeing" him a lot lately. There was the bus the other day, and a week before that, a queue at the supermarket checkout. Surely that's all this was.

"Sorry," Maggie said, straightening up. She shook her hair out, which she'd just had cut in a severe bob, before she opened her eyes, trained them at the table ahead and saw George. *Fuck. Fuck, fuck, fuck!* Her ankle gave way.

"Need someone to lean on?" Florence said, took her elbow, and led her directly to George, who apparently was now Lionel, and introduced him as her boyfriend. "Finally, my two favorite people meet!"

George, to his credit, smiled warmly, but gave nothing away. His hair was longer, slightly curly the way it got in the rain. His skin was tanned, as if he'd been surfing every day in his new life. *With Florence. How? How could this be?*

"The infamous Maggie." He stood, went in for her cheek while she braced herself against the swoon that overtook her, the same reaction she always had when he had touched her all those years ago, and then, thankfully, embraced her for a moment while she tried to recover. *George! How could Florence's boyfriend—the one she's been waiting to have pop the question—be George? My George?*

When he disentangled himself, he looked right into her eyes and her throat went dry recalling the dream she'd had earlier that week about just that look, followed by one of his erotic kisses. She tried to blink the image away.

Now was the moment. Own up to it, put it out there. *We used to date.* Laugh over the awkwardness and then move on. They were all adults.

"Where's Reg?" Florence asked before she could think of anything at all to say. George/Lionel scanned the room. Just at that moment Reg came huffing around that same winding route she'd followed the Amazonian hostess along moments prior.

Maggie did her best to smile as she palmed in Reg's direction. When he caught her eye, she could tell he was angry. She shouldn't have left him, and she couldn't exactly explain why she had, but now she had bigger problems.

"I've been calling you, Maggie! You didn't tell me which restaurant it was. There were five right where we got out of the taxi." He was nearly yelling.

"Florence, Riley, this is Reg," she said. Of course she'd told him which restaurant. But what was the point?

Instinctively, she looked into George's eyes, it was as if they'd made some silent agreement: they would not tell. It would be too awkward, or hard, or whatever. Forget that thing about being adults. Instead, she thought, they would take it to their graves. That would be much better.

One-click to buy this book and continue reading now!

ABOUT THE AUTHOR

Daniella Brodsky writes sexy, swoony romance with hot alphas, often in far-off destinations. This is because she's lived all over, from New York to London to Sydney and Honolulu. She lives in Australia, and lots of her alphas are Aussie because let's face it: they're hot. The accent doesn't hurt either. That's why she married one.

Want a free book? Sign up for Daniella reader's group. You'll also get new release info, giveaways, and sales. www.daniellabrodsky.com.